BATTLE
EARTH X

NICK S. THOMAS

First published in the United Kingdom
by Swordworks Books.

ISBN 978-1-911092-14-8

Typeset by Swordworks Books
Printed and bound in the UK & US
A catalogue record of this book is available
from the British Library

Cover design by Swordworks Books
www.swordworks.co.uk

BATTLE
EARTH X

NICK S. THOMAS

PROLOGUE

From Colonel Mitch Taylor's personal journal - Uncharted space, Day 5

Leaving Earth has changed each person differently. We haven't even been gone a week, and men and women are tearing themselves apart at every level of our new found society.

I needed Jones to be at my side as we drove forward into a new era for humanity, and his loss is one of the greatest. We beat Karadag, we beat Demiran; no one ever imagined we could be beaten so quickly by Erdogan. He is a new breed of enemy, unlike any we have seen before.

Earth fell, and we have been cast adrift in the universe. But we are alive. We will return to Earth. I don't know when, and I don't know how, but we will take our home back.

CHAPTER ONE

The crowds were still cheering from Taylor's triumphant and hopeful speech when warning lights flashed on several consoles across the bridge. The cheering quickly curtailed as the ensign yelled, "We've got multiple hull breaches, Sir!" Taylor rushed to the ensign's console to see the locations himself on a blueprint screen of the massive vessel.

"Are we under attack?" Huber asked bluntly.

Taylor looked up grimly. "Bet your ass. Those aren't random. We've got five breaches at least, and hard to tell how many more as your security systems falter. We've got unwelcome guests, lot's of 'em."

Huber opened a comms channel throughout the ship.

"This is the Admiral speaking. We..."

"Sir," the ensign interrupted, "We've lost all comms. Weapon systems are down, engines, too..."

"What the hell is going on?"

"They're dismantling your ship," replied Taylor.

"It'll be chaos. Few of the crew are armed and ready to fight those things."

"What emergency communication do you have?"

"Without power?" Huber asked, "Light beacons, that's it."

"Taylor turned to the comms officer."

"Put out this message."

The officer looked over to Huber for confirmation. The Admiral simply nodded for him to comply, but Taylor had already continued relaying the message.

"Enemy forces aboard. Do not approach or attempt to make contact in any way, and keep repeating it."

"We could call on some of the Marine ships for assistance?" Huber asked.

"Negative. We have no idea how bad this situation is for us or any other vessel in the fleet. We need to resolve this ourselves and quickly. Where is your officer of the watch?"

"Here!" a hesitant voice shouted.

Taylor looked around and found a young female officer. She was almost shaking in fear and shock.

"Your job is to put the word out. Send runners if you have to. Ensure all aboard know what to expect and are appropriately armed and prepared for it."

"What should they expect, Sir?" she asked.

"All hell to break loose. We've almost certainly got

Mechs aboard and in some number. Get to it."

"Aye, aye, Sir," she replied.

The officer rushed off with the utmost urgency, now she had some task to work on. Huber had brought up a 3D projected model of the ship before them, with all known breaches marked.

"We've still got some power, then?" Taylor asked.

"Life support and basic systems, but that's about all," replied the ensign.

Taylor signalled for Jafar to step up beside them.

"What are they planning?"

He looked at the 3D map for just a few short seconds before replying bluntly, "Have they destroyed the ships weapon systems?"

"No," replied Huber, "Just disabled our power."

"Then they intend to seize the weapons for themselves."

"To what end?"

"Maximum destruction of the fleet."

"They've already got our guns. All they'd have to do is seize the bridge, and they'd manage it," Huber gasped.

"That's not gonna happen," Taylor said confidently.

He could tell Huber didn't look so confident.

"Parker!" Taylor roared.

Sergeant Eli Parker rushed up to him.

"You and your platoon are staying put. You stop any of those bastards getting in here? Got it?"

She nodded in agreement, rushing off to gather her

unit.

"And get Dubois in here. You keep her safe now."

"Got it!" she yelled and she continued on.

He looked out at two-dozen of the Inter-Allied troops who had come aboard with him. They were laying about the entrance. He quickly noticed Corporal Robinson and was surprised to see he had made it.

"Corporal, amongst Jones' Company that came aboard, who is the most senior?"

He shrugged for a moment and then responded, "I guess I am."

"You've got about platoon strength. They're yours now. Do the Captain proud."

His face went blank in disbelief, but he accepted it in a dignified fashion.

"Platoon leaders, get your asses here now."

The remaining three, including Corporal Robinson stepped up and joined him and the Admiral. Lieutenants Matthews and Anders. Both men promoted up from the ranks that Taylor had gotten too little time to get to know as officers. All he knew was they were hardy enough fighters to have made it that far with him. Jafar still stood and listened in, and Morris joined them.

"What can I do?" asked the former MDF Captain.

Taylor had forgotten he was even still with them. He had blended into the grunts throughout the operation. Taylor knew the former Moon colonist had no idea if his people had made it out alive, and yet here he was doing everything he could to help.

"You stick with me," replied Taylor.

Morris did not protest. It was clear he was not going to wrestle for any kind of command or leadership capacity. Taylor pointed to the lower decks of the ship. "Anders, here. Matthews you'll take the port side. I'll sweep the starboard decks."

"And the centre?" Huber asked.

"Your people are gonna have to take up some of the slack. We're in communication blackout. For most of the crew that means they're on their own; mostly lightly equipped and probably unaware of the enemy presence. Lives are at stake here, and every second we waste will be more lives lost. Jafar, you stay here."

The alien looked surprised, but Taylor merely glared at him, and he did not protest. Taylor knew he was his strongest asset, and he needed that asset protecting the bridge.

"And me?" Silva asked.

"On me," he replied.

He fully intended to sweep quickly through the ship, and he wanted the Sergeant Major by his side. He looked around the bridge to see few of the crew knew what they could or should be doing. Most had little control over the systems they were tasked with monitoring. He leaned in close to Huber.

"You've got weapons lockers nearby?"

"Yes."

"Then draw everything you can. Get a gun in every one of their hands, and be ready for a fight."

Huber was taken aback. It was clear he had never had to fight with his own hands before, despite being a competent naval officer and commander.

"You can stop them, can't you?"

"We have to."

Taylor turned and headed for the door where Parker was now waiting with her platoon.

"Come on, let's move!"

He tapped Parker on the shoulder as he rushed past without a word and grabbed a shield that lay propped up with others at the entrance.

Here we go again, he thought.

"Any idea on their number?" Silva asked.

"No idea," he replied.

They quickly took a turn and headed for the start of the areas he had designated for his platoon.

"Lot of ship to cover," Silva commented.

"Sure is."

They carried onwards and stumbled across three crewmembers walking the decks as if it were any other day.

"We've been boarded. Get to cover," said Taylor. He wanted to yell at them but knew he had to keep his voice down. The three crew and stopped and looked at them in shock, but as they looked past Taylor to the line of marines at his back, they began to take his words more seriously and rushed off without another word.

"Think Kelly made it with us?" Taylor asked of Morris.

"Off Earth, or into wherever the hell we are now?"

Taylor shrugged. "Either, I guess."

"Commander Kelly believed in the Exodus, but it doesn't mean he wasn't stubborn enough to stay put and fight it out on Earth."

"You think he'd do that?"

"You nearly did."

Taylor nodded in agreement as they continued on. He couldn't help but feel sorry for Morris. They had all walked away from their lives, but most had brought at least some friends and family with them. What did Captain Morris have? He had evacuated his home for the second time, and probably left everyone he knew to an all but certain death.

"You want a job in the Regiment?" Taylor asked him.

He looked back to see Morris shrug.

"We're the closest thing you have got to family in...well, wherever we are. I know you are up to the task. Keep your rank. I need solid officers right now. What do you say?"

"I'm in. Just as long as you know it's only until such time I can get back to my own people."

"Sure."

Morris nodded in gratitude, and Taylor could see a little relief in his eyes, but there was no time to dwell on it. Gunfire erupted nearby, and they were not human weapons. Taylor rushed on to find an intersection, with pulses smashing into a position where three naval crewmembers were huddled back behind a few crates. The range was shortening as their attackers advanced on them. One of the crew put a pistol out from cover and fired a few blind shots, but they had little hope of doing damage even if they found a target.

The crew hadn't even noticed his arrival under the hail of gunfire. One had his head in his hands and was frozen solid in panic and shock. Taylor reached down for a grenade but found his webbing empty.

Shit, he thought to himself.

The gunfire was close now, and he had to act. He did the only thing he could think to do. He rushed out from the cover of their corridor and charged towards the source of the gunfire.

A few seconds later, he stormed past the crew who still hadn't noticed their presence over the noise of the impacts landing all about them. As the creatures came into view, he saw the nearest was one of the heavily armoured line breakers, but he did not have any option but to head right for it. Two pulses smashed into his shield, and he fired repeatedly as he advanced. Every single one of his shots was absorbed by the Mech's heavy armour until finally he dropped his rifle and drew his Assegai.

Mitch hit the creature with his shield head on, and with all the power his body and exoskeleton suit would afford him. The creature slid back half a metre and then came to a dead stop.

Oh, shit!

He felt his shield being yanked forward as the creature took a hold of it, lifted him up, and smashed him into the ceiling like a ragdoll. He winced in pain from the impact but managed to keep hold of his weapon. A moment later the Mech's massive spear-like weapon was driven up through his shield and pierced the ceiling. It just skimmed the flank of his armour. Gunfire rushed past beneath him, as Morris and the others fired under him to try and take the beast down. They had little effect, but it was enough to give him an opening.

He let go of the shield, for he had no chance of getting away from the alien's grasp, and rolled off behind the Mech. As he descended, he thrust his Assegai into its back. It penetrated deep into the armour; the Mech spasmed and straightened its back. He hit the ground and watched the Mech then become limp and collapse down before him. He turned just in time to see the barrel of a pulse cannon in his face. He rotated around and out of the way of the shot.

As he did so, he drew his pistol and fired three shots into the Mech, but they did little as they found the thickest of its armour. The alien pivoted the gun around for a second shot, but as it did, it was struck by a dozen Reitech rounds and killed where it stood. He looked back to Morris' position, in time to see a grenade fly past him, and he heard the words, "Get down!"

Mitch collapsed down to the deck, using the cover of the dead Mech to shield him. A moment later, a blinding flash ignited the corridor. He felt the blast rush past, and fragments striking his helmet and shoulder armour. From his position, he reached over for the Assegai in the dead Mech and drew it out in readiness. He kept his head down, as friendly gunfire raced overhead for almost half a minute, and then all went silent. He felt something touch his shoulder. He turned quickly in shock to see Silva was kneeling down beside him.

"Anyone ever told you you're a crazy son of a bitch, Sir?" he asked with a smile.

"Not recently."

The Sergeant Major helped him to his feet, and he picked up his shield that had been bent around his body, and still had the alien's spear embedded. He put his foot on the surface and pulled the shaft until the blade prised back out. He looked at the weapon for a moment. It was as he had first thought, little more than a double sized version of their Assegais. It was unwieldy compared to his, but felt like it could do wicked damage on impact from its sheer size and breadth alone.

Mitch laid his shield flat to look at the gaping hole which had nearly been his death. The steel had folded in and been penetrated like tin. Three leaves stuck up from where the metal had been forced apart and left a huge hole. He knew it wouldn't do to use it in that state. He turned the enemy spear around and smashed down at the shield where it was damaged; and hammered the damaged parts back down flat so that they almost touched one another once more.

It was a desperate measure, but he'd rather have a damaged shield than none at all. He threw the enemy weapon aside in disgust and looked up at the others who had been fixated on his bodge of a field repair.

"You find a better one along the way, you let me know," he said to them.

He remembered the Navy crew and pushed his way through to reach them. They hadn't moved from their cover. They were too terrified to do anything at all, and had nothing but a single sidearm between them.

"The ship is under attack. Either get somewhere safe or draw weapons and fight," he said to them, "Carry on like this, and you'll be dead before the day is out."

"What...what can we do against those things?" one of them stammered.

"What we have been doing since this began. Give them everything you've got. Now move!"

He grabbed one of them and hauled them out from

cover, and the other two followed. "Go!" he yelled at them.

"You know they won't survive two seconds if they run into another Mech?" Morris asked.

"Yeah, and none of us will last much longer if we don't get this situation under control."

A Mech lying seemingly dead beside him began to move, but he quickly responded by kicking it back down and then driving his foot into the faceplate three times until it cracked, and he crushed the creature's head inside.

"Next time you put one of these things down, you be sure to finish the job," he said to the Captain.

With that, he lifted his shield back up from the floor and continued onwards.

* * *

Parker stood at the entrance to the bridge, looking out to the improvised barricades her platoon had assembled a few metres out into the corridor. She knew the blast doors would seal the bridge for a while, but not forever. They had to be prepared to defend the main access corridor, should they come under attack. Her visor was up so that she could use the ship's air supply rather than that of her suit. She could feel the sweat dripping down her face. The air conditioning systems were obviously running at minimal power, but it was stress and concern as much as the heat that made her perspire so much.

She knew Taylor would be fine. He always seemed to make it out okay. It was the rest of them she was concerned for. She turned back to look for Coco Dubois. Jones' wife sat propped up against one of the bridge consoles. She had a pistol in one hand resting in her lap. Her eyes wandered and she was in a daze. She had the look of absolute loss that Parker had seen so often in the war.

She walked over to Dubois and knelt down beside her, although she had no clue what, if any, words could consul her after all she had lost.

"How you doing?" It was all she could think to say.

Dubois shook her head, but it wasn't clear if that meant 'not well' or she simply didn't want to answer, but Parker waited for one anyway. She stared long enough that she finally got a response.

"Everything I have ever known is gone. My husband, my regiment, my country, everything."

Huber had heard, as well as several other of the crew. It was hard not to in the suspenseful silence which had overcome the bridge since Taylor had left.

"What is the point of this anymore?" she asked them, "What are we even doing here all huddled together, hoping we can live today and die another day not far from now?"

Parker was not at all surprised by her words, but she could see it was only serving to continue fuelling the fire of fear that all around them were feeling. She was finally overcome by anger as she thought of the bitter price they had paid, and her sympathy turned to disgust.

"Is that how you choose to remember Captain Jones?" she snapped.

Dubois looked at her in surprise with her mouth open and unable to respond.

"Is that how you choose to remember one of the greatest defenders of the human race? He died so that you, all of us, could live. And we are gonna bloody live! You think this is the first loss anyone has ever had? Nations have been defeated, peoples have been scattered to the winds before. This is life. This is our life! So quit feeling sorry for yourself and start acting like who you are; who we all are. We are fighters. Survivors. It doesn't matter what nation you're from, which army, navy. We're in this together, and we are the lucky few!"

Huber hadn't said a word to stop her; despite the fact, the Sergeant had ultimately addressed the entire bridge. Her words were humbling, and he could not help but listen and agree. Dubois looked sheepish and a little embarrassed, although Parker could see Dubois was just as angry with her as she was understanding. Finally, Huber stood up tall and added some words of his own.

"Listen to this Sergeant. She speaks the words we all need to hear! This is all a lot to take in. But we owe it to all those we lost and left behind to make this work. Even now, our people are fighting through this vessel to protect us. So we haven't got it so bad. I don't want to see any more tears. I don't want any more panic. This is the USS Washington, flagship of the fleet, and you are her crew. Start acting like it!"

As he finished, a voice shouted from the corridor, "Here they come!"

It was followed by gunshots as Parker's platoon began laying down fire, and she rushed to the doorway to see for herself. The crew looked to Huber, who was the only one of the bridge crew still standing defiantly and seemingly without regard for the danger. He picked up a rifle that lay on the operations table beside him.

"Don't fear them. They are nothing but an infection that must be cured. We've made it this far. Don't fall now. Pick yourselves up, and protect this ship and all aboard it with everything you've got. All that hatred and anger you feel, vent it at those things out there!"

He didn't get much of an enthusiastic response, but a few at least got up from the cover they had leapt to and stopped cowering down. Parker got to the barricade and could see Mechs advancing at them with breaching shields much like they carried. Their gunfire wasn't getting through in any sort of quantity.

Dozens of shots hit the heavy wall of shields and did little at all. Parker froze, trying to think of what to do. She knew she couldn't use grenades so close to the bridge and so many of the vital systems around them.

"Concentrate fire at their feet!" she shouted.

She was the first to do so, and the first few shots hit the deck and glanced off one of the creature's shield, but one seemed to make it up and through. A few others followed suit, and the Mech was forced to lower its shield to cover its advance. Just as it did, and creating an opening to its head, Jafar took a well-aimed shot. It hit the Mech's head, and two other shots followed it but neither penetrated.

"Their armour is too thick up front. We're gonna have to do this hand-to-hand!" Parker hollered.

She knew the Assegai was the most powerful weapon in their arsenal, for those who were both brave and unfortunate enough to be forced to use it. She let her rifle sling down at her side, drew out her Assegai in readiness, and continued to stay covered by their barricade. The sound of a Mech crashing down flat on the deck told her they had taken one down, but it was a small result for the amount of fire they had to lay down.

Parker stood up to look over the defences, but she realised too late that the first Mech was already on them. It struck the barriers without slowing down and smashed them aside. She ducked down just in time so that the creature barrelled over her rather than taking the force head on. As she got to one knee, the second line was already on her, and she had to deal with it, relying on those behind her to take on the first rank that had gone over the top of her.

A spear was coming right for her. As she parried it

aside, stepping out of much of the power of the blow, she noticed one of her own lying lifelessly at her feet, his neck snapped from the impact of the attack. It had distracted her long enough that the creature's shield came hurtling towards her, losing her any opportunity she had to strike.

Parker barely managed to get her shield in front of her when she was struck by the door-like equivalent carried by the Mech. The energy lifted her off her feet and launched her back against the sidewall. It stopped her violently and shook her a little. As she tilted her shield aside to get a view of her attacker, she saw something dart out from the corner of her eye. It was Jafar launching himself onto her attacker. He drove his Assegai deep into the creature's lead arm, forcing it to drop its weapon.

The Mech responded by swinging its shield edge violently towards him, but the nimble alien ducked under and drove his weapon into its upper leg, dealing a finishing blow through a weak point in the joint under its right arm.

"Get down!" a voice roared.

Parker looked back at their line, and it was three deep, as if to fire like a musket salvo. She felt something grasp her back and knew it was Jafar pushing them both to the ground. The corridor lit up as the slaughter began, and gunfire soared over her head in a seemingly unbroken and continuous stream. After a few seconds, she turned to look at the Mechs being cut down one after the other. Only the first two ranks had been equipped with the heavy boarding equipment that had proven so difficult to damage.

She watched as they fell until ten Mechs lay dead before her and several behind. The sound of gunfire finally died down, and she got to her feet. She stood over the body of one of the creatures and stabbed down through its helmet, running her blade to the hilt. She then proceeded through the lines of bodies to do likewise. As she reached the last one, she looked back to the gun line and saw it was Huber who had ordered her down to cover. The Admiral himself was among them and reloaded his rifle as she approached.

"That was just one boarding party! Maybe even just one stick. Reload, and let's get this barricade back up!" she ordered.

Jafar dragged a Mech body to the line and stacked it up along with the crates they had been using. A few of the navy personnel looked in horror at the sight, but for the men and women of the Inter-Allied Regiment, it was a necessity of survival they had long come to accept as part of day-to-day life. He used the huge enemy shields to bolster the defence, and their bodies to hold them up either side, before once again taking up position behind them.

"So this is what it has come down to?" Huber asked, "Every single one of us fighting with our bare hands for one last gasp chance of survival. Is this what the end looks like?"

"This isn't the end. I say it isn't. I choose that it isn't, so don't let it be so," she replied.

* * *

A trail of blue drips followed Taylor as the enemy blood still poured from his boot. He carried on as if not even noticing.

"We're not far from the main weapon controls grid," he whispered.

As he said it, they saw the bodies of four marines ahead and several other of the navy crew scattered about them. Two Mechs lay dead amongst them. Taylor shook his head.

"Idiots, we can't afford those kind of losses."

"Looks like they put up a fight," replied Morris.

"Not much of one," he spat back, "If those are the kind of losses we can expect, then we might as well give up now."

Taylor increased his pace; knowing time was not on their side. A moment later, they heard the ship power up, and all remaining lighting come on. It revealed the extent of the bloodshed around them, but Taylor knew that didn't matter right now. He put a direct call through to the bridge.

"This is Taylor. Someone speak to me."

The response finally came, and it was far more casual than he had expected, but it was good to hear a voice.

"Taylor, how's it going out there?" Huber asked.

"We're not far from the weapons grid control point now. Looks like power is back up, and you?"

"Negative, nothing's changed our end."

"That's not good."

"What do you mean?"

"The Krys took out our power for a reason. If they've just returned it, then it must be because they've got what they wanted."

Over the comms channel Taylor could hear an alarm sound, and frantic voices followed.

"What's going on, Admiral?"

He had to wait for a response.

"Weapon systems are powering up. Oh, God! They could wipe out half the fleet. Colonel, you must get to them. Stop our weapon systems before they are ready to fire!"

"How long have I got?"

"The core reboot and calibration of weapons can take up to two minutes. That's all you have."

"Got it, Taylor out."

Shit!

"Two minutes until those bastards fire on our own. No time to play this cautious. Let's move!"

He leapt forward into a running pace and had to rush right over the top of fallen soldiers from both sides. He went forward now without a care for his own life. He well understood the thousands of lives that would be lost if he did not complete his mission. He took the bend up ahead and instantly spotted four Mechs standing guard at their final destination, but he did not stop or hesitate.

Pulses raced towards him from the creatures concentrating their fire. He fired his rifle as he closed the distance and killed one with a lucky shot, but two carried shields and firearms in the same way his own marines did. As he got halfway, he felt his shield buckle, and the heat transfer was becoming unbearable. He fought through it and kept going until the shield shattered into three parts and dropped from his arm.

As it did, Taylor leapt into a roll. Pulses flew overhead, and he came up to one knee in front of the first creature. With his left hand, he took hold of the barrel of its pulse cannon and held it up so that the shots dispersed into the roof above. He then raised his rifle and placed the barrel against the creatures' stomach, holding the trigger until the magazine was empty. He let go his firm grasp, and the Mech dropped dead before him. His glove was smoking from the burn on the heat shield of the weapon, and he could feel his skin cooking beneath the reinforced fabric.

A Mech spear came at him as he got to his feet. He could only step aside to avoid it and drew out his Assegai. The creature lunged at him again, but in doing so exposed its flank. Taylor's comrades took their opportunity and opened up with a devastating barrage of fire. The alien stumbled back against the frame of the doorway they were protecting and collapsed in front of the Colonel.

The final Mech turned to face the vicious salvo and absorb the impact with its shield, but now it was Taylor's chance. He jumped towards the alien, without it even noticing under the weight of fire and unable to move. He drove his Assegai deep into its flank. It reacted quickly by swinging its shield around to strike him. Taylor was quick to respond but didn't clear the distance quick enough.

The impact smashed his shoulder back and nearly tore it out of its socket. But as he winced in pain, he saw the creature spasm with the impact of a dozen shots riddling its body. He felt he's knees go a little weak until Silva's steady hold kept him up.

"Let's finish this."

Taylor nodded in response and turned to see two of his people placing charges on the door.

"Ready to breach, Sir."

"Do it."

He reached down and picked up a massive alien shield that was as tall as he was. The charges blew; their shaped charges being comparatively short and quiet, and blowing the door open in one. Taylor leapt ahead and was the first through the breach. He was propping the weighty shield up with his other hand that still carried his Assegai and sprinted forward.

The shield had transparency to a large upper section, allowing him to stay covered while advancing. He could see a pulse rushing to his head, but he continued at a rapid pace, under the assumption the shield would be defence enough against the alien weapons.

Taylor didn't break stride but hit the Mech full force at a sprinting pace. It lifted off its feet, smashing down on the deck, as he clumsily rolled over and landed the other side of the creature. From the floor, he reached back and drove his Assegai into its head before it could get back up, killing it with a single blow. As he drew it out, the blood sprayed across his armour, and he saw Silva and the rest rush past, guns blazing.

But then his heart almost stopped when he heard what he had prayed he would not. The Washington's weapons batteries began firing, and they could be felt and heard throughout the entire ship. He didn't have to say a word. They all knew what was at stake. He jumped to his feet and followed on behind the cover of his platoon. They advanced on the main control panels where three Mechs now defended.

"Take them down! Take the fuckers down!" he yelled.

One of the marines beside him was struck in the face by a pulse and dropped dead, but he didn't even get to see who it was. There was no time. As they approached, the sheer weight of fire was knocking the last few creatures back out of their cover. He saw his moment and pushed his way to the front, leaping on the nearest creature to end it quickly. He stabbed it five times into the abdomen until it collapsed towards him. He brushed it aside.

Taylor instantly turned to the consoles that Silva and Morris had managed to reach.

"I can't turn this off," said Morris.

"What do you mean, you can't?"

"They've programmed it with something. We're locked out."

"Who can unlock it?"

"Ship's engineers, I guess, but it could take them hours."

"Not good enough!" Taylor shouted.

He thought for just a second before grabbing Morris and hauling him aside. As he did, he ripped the officer's rifle from his hands and took aim at the console with it. He didn't hesitate for a second before firing full auto into the computer console, and then turning to the other and fired until there was nothing left but twisted metal and burnt out components.

As his rifle went silent, they waited, listened, hoped, and then heard it. The weapons stopped. Morris gave out a sigh of relief.

"How did you know that would work?"

"I didn't."

CHAPTER TWO

Taylor strode towards the bridge, but when he took the final turn, a shot from one of their weapons struck the wall beside him. He stopped, looking to see it had come from one of the crewmembers beside Parker at the barricade ahead. He saw her backhand the perpetrator.

Bodies lay atop one another, and he had to tread in an ungainly fashion from one to another. He reached Parker. Her cheek was bleeding where a few pieces of shrapnel had cut into her flesh, but she was still standing, and that was all he needed to know.

The defenders split apart and allowed him to pass where he found Huber sitting beside his operations table, with his rifle next to him. He did not have the look of a man who had successfully held onto his ship.

"We have secured all system control points. We're just carrying out final sweeps of any stragglers. This is over,"

Taylor stated.

Huber nodded and sighed as if there was no relief in the news at all.

"You didn't get to them in time," he muttered.

Taylor took offence to the comment.

"Yes we did, Sir!"

The Admiral turned in surprise but could not get a word out as Taylor carried on.

"We stopped the weapon systems as fast as was humanly possible. We saved all the lives that could be saved, so don't you start calling this a failure. Whatever, and whoever, we lost to our own weapon systems was tragic, but let's not forget who the enemy is. Let's not forget who fired those weapons. We cannot afford to turn on one another and blame one another when this is all we have left!"

The Admiral nodded in agreement as Taylor approached.

"I don't like losing a single soul anymore than you do, but let's get real here. This is a war. We may have escaped it for a while, but we are going to keep losing people until we have won."

"Won? You think we can win this?" Huber whispered.

"Fuck yeah. And if you don't believe it too, we have no chance."

Taylor was speaking quietly, but it was still carrying throughout the room. Everyone stood and listened. Taylor took a step closer and whispered to Huber.

"They need you. So what do you say? Will you fight for

this?"

Huber nodded in agreement, and Taylor stepped back for him to address the crew.

"We've got people that need our help. I want emergency crews out there now, doing what they can. All crews are to be escorted by marines until further notice. Let's get to work!"

He looked to his XO, Captain Vega. "See to it."

"Aye, aye, Sir," he replied, calmly moving to take control of the situation.

"What are our losses? What sort of damage was done?" Taylor asked of the Admiral.

"One frigate, the Valiant destroyed, severe damage to a Destroyer, the Tuscon, and one of the barges destroyed."

"Completely?"

Huber nodded and brought up a small display screen so that only the two of them could see. Taylor saw thousands of little bits of debris floating in space. It was only as Huber zoomed in a little that he could see many of those pieces of debris were actually bodies.

"There were up to twenty thousand souls aboard that ship. Gone, just like that, and at the hands of our own weapon systems. This happened on my watch, and I will never forgive myself."

"You take that anger, and you vent it somewhere else. You are the leader of this fleet, and perhaps the de facto leader of the human race. You do not have the luxury of feeling that guilt."

Taylor rested against the table and took off his helmet, placing it beside him. He tried to think about the next step. It was hard to even imagine what life now had in store for them. He looked up. His own people looked to him for direction now, just as did many of the ship's crew.

"First things first," said Taylor, "Where the fuck are we?"

He looked to the Admiral, who in turn looked to his navigation officer who was as speechless as the rest of them. Eventually, Taylor looked to Jafar, who had not spoken up yet.

"You said you would choose our final destination. That is what you told me, wasn't it? That you would know and no other until we made it through?"

Jafar slowly nodded in agreement.

"Then start talking."

All eyes turned to the alien. They did not stare in contempt or distrust now, but in curiosity. They wanted to hear what he had to say, and they were willing to believe it, no matter what. They simply wanted answers.

"Well, are you gonna share, or what?" Taylor asked.

"Maybe this is better done in private," added Huber.

"No," he replied and pointed to the crew, "They have all sacrificed enough and given enough to be deserving of answers. I won't keep them from it now."

The Admiral nodded in agreement.

"All right, let's hear it..."

He stopped abruptly, not sure how to address the alien.

"Jafar is a Sergeant in my unit," Taylor prompted him.

"Sergeant Jafar..."

"I plotted a course for us to the only place I knew they would not be, and the last place they would want to go to pursue us. No Krycenaean would ever choose to come to this place. "

"Why?" Taylor asked.

"This system is called...what can only be translated as the 'Death Space'. To the Krys it is a kind of hell mixed with the myth of your Bermuda Triangle. Those who come here never return."

"And you brought us here?" Huber asked sternly.

Taylor lifted his hand to stop the Admiral as he stormed towards Jafar. The Admiral first took offence, but then calmed himself.

"So where the hell is this place?" he spat.

"With the correct maps, I should be able to show you, but it is not where we are that need concern you, but what the place is."

"And what is that?"

"In truth, I do not know."

"You what?"

"You'd better start talking some sense," added Taylor, "as this is starting to sound like crazy talk."

"Yes, it is, and always was," Jafar replied.

Taylor strode across the room and leaned in close to whisper to Jafar.

"Look at these people. They are ready to give up. You need to give them something. Make them know we are safe."

"But I do not know that we are."

"I don't give a shit. You brought us here, and you must have had some pretty good reasons for doing so. Make them understand, and better still, help me understand."

He looked into Jafar's eyes as the alien thought it over and finally nodded once in agreement. Taylor took a few paces back and let him continue.

"This place is feared by all of my race. Rumours and myths surround it. I do not know how many if any are true. All I know is that no Krys has ever gone there in my lifetime and returned."

"And why would that be?" Huber asked, "Don't you think whatever makes it so dangerous to your people might be equally so for us?"

"Maybe, but it cannot be worse than the alternative. There is no other place I know where Erdogan would not find us and bring an end to us all."

Huber shook his head. "I'm hearing a whole lot about what you don't know about this place, what do you know?"

"Nothing that is fact."

Taylor could see there was something Jafar was wary of telling them, almost fearful. He wanted to press him on it but knew it was neither the time nor the place.

"Is that all you have for us?" asked the Admiral, "So let me get this straight. You have taken us to a ghost system, which could well contain dangers that could bring about our end, and you cannot tell us anymore?"

"Yes."

"Well, that's just great. We trusted you. We entrusted the human race to you, and you have failed us."

"And what else would you have had him do?" Taylor interrupted, "He is not a miracle worker. If you could have picked a location, where would you have gone?"

"Anywhere that I knew wasn't enemy controlled, or somewhere called the... Death Space or whatever it is."

"Erdogan's influence stretches across vast swathes of the galaxy as you or I know it. Anywhere you would have chosen would only likely have contained Krys forces or long distance scanners and drones that would have had the same effect," added Jafar.

Huber turned to the alien and opened his mouth to speak but stopped, realising Jafar may have made the best of a list of bad options.

"We're here now," Taylor said firmly, "and most significantly, we are alive. Let's not forget how valuable that is and keep going forward."

The XO stepped back aboard, and Huber took it as an opportunity to speak.

"Where are we up to?" asked Huber, "I want an update

on all systems."

Vega rushed to his console. He clearly already had an overview because he began talking before he reached it.

"Power has returned to most systems. Engines and weapon systems are active. Life support is holding, but we still have fires on two levels, and several sectors have had to be isolated due to hull breaches. We have crews working as fast as they can, but it's taking time while the marines ensure they can work in safety. Sweeps of the ship are ongoing."

"All right, good work. I want a full report of casualties across the fleet."

Huber turned towards Taylor but stopped, looked back to Vega, and hesitated before asking. "And a full headcount of the fleet. Let's see how many remain of the human race."

It was a gruelling thought and a tough question to ask, but they needed to know.

"Sir, I'm getting readings of something…"

They all turned to the comms officer carefully studying a display before him.

"What the hell is it?" Vega asked.

"A manmade, or… something not naturally made structure, Sir. It's the nearest object in space to our position."

Vega rushed to the officer's side and studied everything before him. Huber and Taylor waited anxiously. They half expected it to be an enemy vessel, but prayed for it not to be.

"It looks like…" Vega started slowly.

"What, speak clearly damn it!" Huber yelled.

"Like a space gateway, and yet… not."

"Shit!" the Admiral shouted and turned to Jafar.

"This is on you. All this bullshit about taking us to safety, and you've landed us right on top of one of their gateways! What the hell are we supposed to do now? We're finished!"

Taylor paced up close to him and leaned in quickly.

"Get a hold of yourself, Admiral. We need your leadership, right now."

"Need? What about what I need? You were in on this, too. What the hell have you done?"

Without any warning, Taylor backhanded Huber. It wasn't especially hard, but the shock was enough to take him off balance, and he stumbled down onto the deck. The XO drew his sidearm and several followed, but Parker and her platoon were as quick to respond with rifles trained on them.

"Put your weapons down!" she screamed.

"You have struck your commanding officer!" Vega yelled at Taylor. He turned to one of his own marines.

"Sergeant, arrest this man. Colonel Taylor, you are under arrest and will cool off in the brig."

The Sergeant didn't move through fear of Taylor and

his own people.

"I gave you an order, Sergeant!" Vega repeated.

"No," replied Taylor calmly in defiance.

He wasn't even holding a weapon, despite the Captain's pistol being training on him. He took a seat on the edge of the operations table but made no attempt to reach for the rifle on top of it.

"I've gone through too much to put up with this crap. You don't like me. I get that. Live with it. I don't want command of this fleet. The Admiral here is quite capable and entitled to the position. But neither will I stand by and see us fall to destruction because of some slackness and weak mindedness."

"So what, you want command?" Vega sneered.

Taylor sighed and yet was as calm as he could be, as all around him were on edge and with fingers on the triggers. He simply shook his head.

"Is this how it will all end? Will humanity not be taken out by an apocalypse or invasion by an alien race? Will we destroy ourselves? Have you not listened to a single word I have said, Captain?"

Vega looked confused and bent down to help the Admiral up when he realised Taylor meant him no harm, or at least appeared to.

"Time to man up, Captain, and that goes for you, too, Sir."

The Admiral looked up at him and into his eyes. Huber's

face had no anger in it, only shame. He had already made some bad calls and appeared weak before the crew. Now he had done it all over again.

"I'm sorry."

Taylor looked surprised. He got up and stepped a little closer to the Admiral, and that made Vega nervous.

"I don't want an apology. I don't want you to say sorry. I don't want you to accept my insubordination. We need you to be the kind of man who doesn't accept weakness, doesn't accept defeat. The kind of Admiral that would be so single minded and focussed that I would be in the brig by now for everything I have just done. It isn't a problem I struck you, Sir, only that you accepted it and have not acted. Get up, and be the man you were always meant to be. Be the Admiral of the fleet."

Huber straightened his uniform and stood up a bit straighter. He began to open his mouth to apologise once again but stopped himself. He smiled and then began to laugh. It broke the ice, and Taylor started laughing with him; many of the troops began to lower their weapons. Finally, Huber raised his right hand to bring silence, and he got it.

"Taylor, you are a son of a bitch, but you are my son of a bitch. You strike me again, and next time you'll not walk."

Taylor grinned at his response, nodding in appreciation as he watched Huber pace confidently across the bridge.

He finally stopped and looked back to Vega.

"Put you weapon down, Captain."

"But, Sir…" he protested.

"Put it down," the Admiral said in a sterner tone but without shouting, "and that goes for the rest of you," he added.

Everyone complied with some relief.

"Let's focus on the task at hand, and that will be our job for every moment of every day we are awake. There is a lot to be done, so let's do it. The space gateway, I want info, now!"

Nobody moved. The Admiral looked around and finally added, "Get to work."

He sounded confident and that confidence projected throughout all of them. Huber and Taylor stared at a projection of the suspected space gateway on the table before them, but it wasn't long before they felt Jafar's presence looming over them. Taylor looked back and could see the same puzzling expression on his friend's face.

"What is it?"

Jafar shook his head.

"This looks somewhat like a jump gate, but not like any I have ever seen."

"Maybe an older pattern?" Taylor asked.

Jafar shook his head. "I do not know."

Well that's fucking great, Taylor thought.

"First thing we need to know is where are we and what are we dealing with? What planets, moons, and threats do we face? These are the questions we need answers to," added Huber. "Taylor, I'll find bunks for you and your people aboard this ship. It won't be pretty, but this is where you need to be right now."

Taylor nodded in agreement. It hadn't even occurred to him that they had no space of their own at all. All they had was what they were wearing. It was a gruelling thought to realise they had quite literally left everything behind.

"I want you to assemble a team to investigate that gateway or whatever the hell it is."

"I'll take two platoons, and I'll need two ships. The Mastiffs we came in on have taken a beating and aren't exactly too flexible."

"You got it, you will be escorted by the Frigate Warrior. She'll keep you safe."

"Thank you, Sir."

"And Taylor," whispered Huber.

"If that gateway shows any sign of opening. Any enemy presence at all, or anything you don't like the look of, you blow it to high hell, you hear?"

"Bet your ass, Sir."

"Take Jafar with you. He's clearly got a better eye than we have for this."

"Aye, aye, Sir."

Taylor could feel exhaustion kicking in, but he knew it

was no time to slacken off.

"Lieutenant Anders, Captain Morris. Gather your platoons and come with me. Where the hell is King?"

"He's en route, Sir," replied Parker.

"Tell him to get half our people into bunks and to get their heads down and rest up. I want the rest cycled through protection details and regular sweeps of the ship."

Parker looked at him in surprise as if to ask why she was being asked to relay a message when their comms were back online.

"Just do it," he repeated.

He carried on past her with Jafar beside him. He realised he was already expecting Morris to fall into line as his right hand man. The Captain was a good man and a solid officer, but he was no replacement for Jones. The loss of his best friend had only gone from his mind in the heat of battle, but now the thoughts of loss flooded back into his head.

"Aysen really owed you so much that he would sacrifice himself like that?" he asked Jafar.

"Is it so hard to believe after what Captain Jones did for us?"

Taylor shook his head.

"That is three of you now, three that have opposed your leaders. It gives me hope."

When Jafar did not respond, Taylor looked around and stared at him to prompt an answer, but one did not come.

"Three of you came over to us, why not more?"

"It was exceptional circumstances which drew us together."

"And that cannot happen again?"

Jafar shrugged.

"One day this war will be over. If we lose, we will likely go to extinction. But if Erdogan loses, we would never wish such an end on his people."

"You would leave them alive, and risk it all happening again?"

"I'm a fighter, like you, not an executioner. If we win this, when we win it, we are gonna have to learn to live with one another. I'd hope some more of your race sees that sooner than later. We are gonna need all the help we can get to return from this."

Taylor could see Jafar was not at all convinced, but he wasn't sure if that was in relation to the Krys living alongside them or the chance of victory. He didn't want to ask. They reached the hangar bay and found Lieutenant Eddie Rains awaiting them.

"So here we are, Colonel. On the raggedy edge of, well, God knows where. But all that matters is..." he turned and pointed, "I got myself a new ride, and she's a sweet one. Mercury T151 combat transport, twice the armour of a copter, pilot controlled weapon systems, and auto targeting turrets top and bottom. She ain't the fastest or the smoothest looking bird out there, but she sure is a bruiser."

Taylor could not help but smile.

"The World may have come to an end, and this is all it takes to perk you up?" he asked Rains.

"Well, hell yeah. I'll take what I can get."

The pilot seemed to genuinely believe his words. Taylor wondered how much of it was a coping mechanism for dealing with all they had endured, and yet, it was working, so he could not criticise it.

"You know our mission?"

"Investigate that gateway, got it."

"We have no idea if that thing is operational or not, or even who it was built by or when, so keep your wits about you. This could be a fact-finding mission, or it could be a trap. Who knows? So you keep alert at all times."

"I always see you home safe, don't I, Colonel?" Rains grinned.

Taylor grimaced. He could think of too many times they had taken a beating and forced to bail or make crash landings.

"All I can say, Lieutenant, is that flying with you if never boring."

Rains laughed.

"Well, I wouldn't want to bore you," he replied, stretching out his hands to invite them aboard, "Step aboard, Gentlemen."

As Taylor paced up the ramp, he saw Rains had painted

the name Gerty beside the cockpit. It was hand-painted and still shining a little as it hadn't fully dried. It brought a smile to his face once again.

The interior was cramped, due to the thickness of the bulkheads and support beams inside, which meant they had to duck under as they got to their seats.

"Not exactly travelling in style, are we?" Taylor asked. Rains was squeezing past them to reach the cockpit.

"Hey, you've got air and a place to park your ass, what more can you ask for?"

"Quite a bit," he replied sarcastically.

A few minutes later they were lifting off from the Washington, and Taylor could just about see out through one of the cockpit windows to the vast fleet before them.

"A lot made it," Rains said.

"A lot didn't."

It was hard to disagree.

"There she is. The Warrior, and what a fine ship she is. Ever thought you'd have a frigate flying in support?"

"No, but then I'd rather like to think we didn't need it."

He turned to Jafar, hoping the alien would share some further knowledge with him.

"So what else do you know about this thing?"

"Nothing," he promptly replied.

"Nothing? I find that hard to believe."

"As I have told you. All I know is what I have experienced and been told by my own people. This I have never seen."

"All right, so these space gateways. Did your people invent the technology?"

He shook his head. "I do not know."

"Well, are there any other races out there you know of who use them?"

"I have heard of such in our history, but they are long forgotten. Defeated by the Krys."

"Defeated? You mean they were made extinct?"

He nodded.

"I just don't get it. Why hunt down a species or people to their very extinction? Why not assimilate them, even use them in some secondary roles, and put them to work or something?"

Jafar shrugged. "I cannot explain it."

"Well, that's a conversation killer," muttered Taylor.

They waited in silence while Rains flew them to the gateway. After an hour, Taylor fell into a daydream, thinking of his time back home between the wars. He remembered the moments he had gotten alone with Eli Parker and then to the seemingly never ending parading around the globe. His staged fights to the cameras didn't seem so bad anymore.

What I'd give to have it all back.

He looked around at the faces of those around them. He didn't have to say a word. Their expressions said all he needed to know. It was the same despair and depression he felt inside. He tried his best to hide it, but it was hard to be convincing.

"How much longer, Eddie?"

"Oh, about two hours."

"Fuck me," he whispered to himself.

Several overheard and nodded in agreement.

Taylor once again fell into a dream, and the time passed quickly now as he visualised Parker's face. Before he knew it, he was being ripped from his pleasant abyss by Rains' voice.

"There she is!"

Taylor looked around in surprise, wondering if those were the first words spoken in the last couple of hours that had gone by, or if he had just tuned everything else out. He stretched to the edge of the small seat and strained his neck to get a better view past the pilot.

"Sure is a big mother," he added.

"What do you make of this?" Taylor asked Jafar, leaning back to let him see.

He took a quick look and then responded, "Nothing more than last time you asked."

Taylor shook his head. "You're a big fucking help."

Jafar seemed to right his back and take offence at the comment before settling down.

"Still not got a full grasp on sarcasm, hey?" Taylor asked.

He looked back to Rains, noting as they approached the structure just how vast and imposing it really was.

"The Warrior, she still with us?"

"Yes, Siree."

"Good, any signs of life?"

"Negative. It looks…well, abandoned."

"What do you mean? Surely the Krys wouldn't leave a gateway like this to rust out and fade away?"

He turned and looked at Jafar to answer him, but the alien only shrugged.

"What do you want me to do?"

"Take us in for a closer look. I want to know for certain what the status of this thing is before we put boots on the ground."

As the words came off his tongue, he realised what a bitter thought that was. Stepping foot on real solid ground seemed like a pipe dream now. It had been less than a day since he had left Earth, but it felt like it could be years before he ever did again.

If ever, he thought.

"Right then, here we go," Rains finally added.

He put power to the reverse thrusters and brought them in quickly but calmly until they were less than fifty metres from the structure.

"What the hell is that?" Rains asked.

On the screens beside him he could see what looked like some kind of lettering across the surface of the ring of the structure.

"That mean anything to you, Jafar?"

Taylor could see the confusion in Jafar's face, and that worried him. It was clear he had never seen them before.

"Those are not Krys symbols. Nor anything I have seen before."

Taylor wasn't sure whether to feel grateful it wasn't Krys, or fearful that another unknown threat now existed.

"Look at this thing," said Rains.

He pointed to damage over multiple parts of the structure.

"Has that been hit deliberately?"

"I'd say more likely it's been hit by space debris, and a lot over a long time period. I think we're looking at some kind of ancient artefact, Mitch."

"What is keeping it where it is?" Morris asked.

The thought hadn't even occurred to Taylor.

"I couldn't say, but it's definitely anchored to this point somehow. What do you want to do?"

"Take us in, Eddie. More than anything right now we need information."

"Well, okay."

He brought them in cautiously towards what looked like some kind of opening ten times the size of their gunship.

"Looks about the best place to put down."

They began their approach, but Taylor was feeling uneasy.

"I don't like this. Old tech of an unknown race, it looks dead, but it's somehow holding its position in space. I don't like it at all."

As he said it, there was a glimmer of movement ahead of them.

"Break, break!" Taylor shouted.

Rains put all power down and banked hard as they saw a dazzling flash ahead of them, and a beam weapon almost the width of their craft narrowly missed them.

"Jesus Christ!" Rains swore under his breath.

He banked again, and another beam rushed past them. As they soared back towards the Warrior, a third beam struck their starboard side and tore off one of the engines and wing. They immediately lost most of their power, went into a spin, and continued to barrel towards the frigate.

Taylor knew they were helpless now and could only hope they would not be hit again. Lighting began to fail, and they lowered their visors, expecting to be blasted into space any second, if they survived at all. The seconds went by, and they felt nothing. Finally, Rains broke the silence.

"Well, that went well."

"What can you do?"

"Nothing, Colonel, it's out of my hands now."

They felt an impact on the ship as if they had collided with something, but there was nothing visible out of the pilot's cockpit until he looked up and could see the lower hull of the other Mercury gunship overhead. They began to slow as they approached the Warrior and they were out of their spin.

"They've got us," Rains said in relief.

None of them said a word as they were escorted to the docking bay of the Warrior. The hatch opened, allowing the access to the ship, and they stepped aboard thankful they were still alive.

"Abandoned my ass, Eddie," said Taylor.

"Hey, I said it looked that way. I'm no expert."

Taylor looked to Jafar. He opened his mouth to ask a question, but he could already see the alien was as surprised by it all as they were.

"Let me guess, you have no more clue than us, right?"

Jafar nodded.

"Where the hell have you brought us?" Morris demanded.

Jafar did not respond, but they all thought it, too. It was hard to think of what else they could have done, but that did not stop them from thinking on it over and over again.

"Wherever the hell we are, it ain't home," said Taylor, "It truly is alien, and we need to start treating it with a little respect and a little caution. That was too close a call."

CHAPTER THREE

Taylor stepped aboard the Washington to find Huber waiting to greet him. As he did so, he could see the badly damaged Gerty being manoeuvred into a repair bay a little further long the landing bay. The Admiral opened his mouth to welcome Taylor aboard, but stopped and stared at the wreck.

"What the hell happened out there?"

"We got our asses kicked is what happened. Whatever that thing is, and whoever it was made by, it ain't too friendly."

"Casualties?"

"Thankfully not, but we came too damn close."

"Well is it hostile, can we expect further trouble?"

The Admiral looked to Jafar, then Rains and Morris, but no one had any answers.

"From what I could tell, we just triggered a self defence

mechanism. My advice, we keep on eye on it, but stay well wide."

"So just ignore it?"

"It's trouble we don't need, right now. It's out there in the middle of nowhere. Who cares? Leave it be."

Huber nodded in agreement. It was just another uncertainty to add to the list of their new location. He paced over to the wrecked ship and Taylor joined him. Rains was close behind them and could only shake his head in despair.

"Just when I thought I'd found my girl for life," he muttered.

"Don't you worry, we'll get her flying again," replied Huber.

Rains was shocked to hear it. "We can't afford to lose a single bird. She'll be patched up and repaired anyway we can," Huber continued.

It wasn't quite the good news Rains had hoped for, as it was such a short term and desperate measure. Huber stopped before the gunship to take a good look over it, but Rains continued on. The Lieutenant carried on until he reached his ship and ran his hand along the fuselage, as though feeling some deep personal connection to it. He located the damage where the wing and engine had been either ripped off or obliterated.

"Look at her. The metal has been melted away like it was nothing at all. Gerty is one of the toughest little birds

I've ever flown, and I've flown a few. But that thing, that weapon. We might as well have had paper walls. If it had hit us dead on, none of us would be here to discuss it."

"It was a damn good bit of flying," Taylor murmured, attempting to reassure him, "damn lucky flying."

Rains slowly turned and looked back to Taylor. His face was pale, and he quivered a little as he responded.

"Luck! How many times can we expect to survive by luck? It can't last forever."

Taylor stepped up and laid his hand on Eddie's shoulder.

"Tough day, but not nearly as tough as it could have been. We all came back alive. Take a few hours. Get some food and sack time. The Admiral is finding us bunks, use them."

Eddie nodded in appreciation and staggered off to do as ordered. Taylor looked around to the others who had gone with him.

"That goes for the rest of you. Get your heads down. Rest, and get some chow. We have a long way ahead of us. I want you ready for anything we have to face!"

None of them moved for a moment.

"Fall out, go!"

They scattered before him, and he was left with Huber and his detail.

"Your people have done some fine work throughout all this, Colonel. Do not think it has gone unnoticed."

"Appreciated, Sir, but we don't ask for anything. All we

want is to win."

Huber looked surprised.

"Win? The battle or the war?"

"Everything," Taylor replied dryly.

With that, he turned and left without as much as a salute to the Admiral or request of leave. Huber did not question it. He felt humbled before the Colonel and knew he would have to rely on him for so many things in the times to come.

Taylor carried on in a weary fashion. Only Morris strode beside him. For a moment he imagined it was Jones walking alongside him, and he turned to make a crack at his British comrade, and then realised it could not be.

"You okay, Colonel?"

Taylor stopped. He was exhausted and wanted nothing more than to lie down where he stood and sleep. But he turned to Morris, who he knew needed a lesson in being an officer within his unit.

"Being okay isn't a luxury we can afford, Captain. Being okay is for the civilians to feel while we protect them. While we fight for the survival of our race so that they can go on living. So that there is still a human race left after all this. So, yes, I am okay. I am okay as any man or woman in the Inter-Allied Regiment is entitled to feel. I am glad to have you with us, Captain, but do not forget your duty."

Taylor turned and left. Morris could not help but feel abandoned and alone. Taylor knew he would, but he was too exhausted to explain it any further. More than that, he knew Morris had a strong will, but not yet strong enough.

He carried onwards. The Washington was roughly familiar to him. He knew where to find the officers' quarters and made his way there. Somehow he expected to have someone guiding him to his quarters, but it never happened. Finally a Sergeant of the marines approached him.

"Can I help you, Sir?"

"Looking for…where I can call home, I guess."

"Sir, your unit are back the way you came and port side. Sector 34F."

He looked surprised and more than a little puzzled. The Sergeant could see it in his face.

"I'm sorry, Sir, but there isn't any accommodation available in the officers' quarters at present. We're already running pretty tight and cycling beds through duty rosters."

"I…uh…see, Sergeant, thank you. Thirty what was it?"

"34F, Sir, it's just…"

"I got it, thanks."

"You okay, Sir?"

He nodded before turning and wandering on. He finally saw a familiar face. Sergeant Silva giving orders to a squad outside the entrance to 34F. He looked as wide-awake and lively as ever.

A good Sergeant Major, thought Taylor.

It was an inspiration to him, too. As he reached Silva,

the others were sent off about their duties.

"Colonel, you look like shit."

"Always the charmer," he replied sarcastically, "This our lot?"

"Yes, Sir, temporary quarters for additional marine contingents. Haven't been used in a few years. Hardly luxurious, but we've had a lot worse. I'm chasing the crew to get you your own quarters, but for now you'll have to rough it with the rest of us."

Taylor nodded in appreciation. He could see Silva was working hard to maintain order. He stepped through into the bunkroom and found it was more basic than he expected. It reminded him of the boot camp when he had first joined the Corps. Beds were built into the walls and three high all the way to the ceiling. The space between each column of beds was just a metre wide, and every three beds a cross roads leading to the others either side.

Reitech armour lay piled up on the floors, as it was too bulky to fit in the narrow lockers beside the beds. It wasn't an old vessel, but it was a sign of how much technology and equipment had changed since it had been laid down. Every bunk in sight was taken. Half the marines filling them were asleep; the others were desperately trying to get to the same state. Few had even taken the time to draw the curtains across for privacy. The light was dimmed anyway, so few cared.

Considering how many of them were awake, it was

eerily quiet, with just one quiet conversation going on in the distance. He carried on down the line until he stopped on finding a small plaque with his name on it beside one of the beds. He looked around to see it was the only one. The bed had been reserved for him. It was a middle bunk and therefore at waist height, for the lowest lay almost on the deck.

Taylor stowed his rifle in the locker and pulled off his armour. But as he opened the curtain to his bed he stopped in surprise to see someone inside. It was Eli, wide-awake and staring at him.

"And I thought this one had been saved for me?" he asked jokingly.

"Oh, it is, as long as you don't mind sharing."

He climbed into the bunk, but even with Eli on her side, they could only just squeeze in, but he didn't care.

"Time to learn how the rest of us live," she said with a smile.

"Sure beats a muddy trench or some bombed out wreck of a town."

"Got that right."

"And anyway, not like you have had to rough it like this in over a decade, Sergeant."

She only smiled in response and cuddled into his shoulder. Taylor was exhausted and falling asleep with seconds of lying down.

"Do you think we'll ever get home? Do you think we'll

ever step foot there again? Stand on real earth and sleep in a proper bed?" she asked.

Taylor at first grumbled and then realised what she had said.

"Damn right we will."

He then nodded off to sleep.

* * *

"They're here! They're here!"

Kelly didn't move or flinch. He knew the enemy was coming and had expected it. The only thing that surprised him was that he was still alive.

"Sir, what the fuck are we gonna do?"

Kelly did not respond.

"Sir!"

Finally, he looked up. It was Doyle; a man who had been with him since it had all began. He turned and looked to Lewis who was sat opposite him in his own home.

"What do we do, Sir?" Doyle asked once again.

"What would you do?"

Doyle was dumbfounded.

"Me?" he answered before a long pause, "Sir, you're the Commander. You are our leader. You must know what to do?"

Kelly shook his head.

"We have to do something," Lewis added.

"We stayed here as to not abandon our home again, but we might as well have gone if we're gonna sit around here and wait to die," said Doyle.

Kelly was trying to consider all their options and could not find an answer or solution.

"There are millions of people left on Earth. We can fight," Doyle said.

"With what? Our infrastructure is gone. What armies are still fighting have been shattered."

"Then we fight them in a different way," said Lewis.

"Kelly looked up at the comms officer desperately wanting to hear an answer to their problems. He was tired of the responsibility that hung so heavily on his shoulders. He didn't say a word, but waited for Lewis to go on.

"We can't win in a straight up fight. So don't. Those bastards see an army, a city, or a stronghold, and they send everything they have at that target and flatten it. So let's not give them that luxury. Let's scatter and hit them where they are weak, and at a time and place of our choosing."

"You're talking about a guerrilla war?"

"Yes, why not? It's worked so many times before, why not? It's that or lay down and die."

Kelly thought about it for a moment. He wondered if he even had the energy left in his body. He was still fit and strong, but he was pushing seventy and weary of it all.

"Sir?" Doyle spoke softly.

Kelly turned to him.

"We've fought, and bled, and lost friends. Lost our colony. But we fought on. We earned the right to be here, to live. Was it all for nothing?"

Kelly shook his head.

"Then what are you waiting for, Sir? The fight is here. It is on us, here and now. If you were going to give up, you should have done it years ago. You've dragged us this far, and I won't let you give up now."

Kelly was utterly surprised by Doyle's words that cut so deeply. He looked to Lewis who only nodded in agreement.

"So you want to fight? Fight, knowing we probably can't win. That we will only prolong ours lives by maybe a few days or weeks?"

"I don't think it's about survival anymore. Taylor and everyone who got off this planet are survivors. I want to hurt those alien bastards. I don't care if I live or die anymore, but I want them to suffer."

Kelly could see the burning hatred in his eyes. It wasn't the best place to work from, but it was better than nothing.

"If we do this, it's going to be bad. It will mean leaving people behind, letting people die. We're gonna have to become something none of us ever imagined. We are going to have to live like wild animals and fight like wild animals," said Kelly.

Doyle nodded.

"I don't think you fully appreciate what life will be like when we go down that path," he added.

"It will be life, which is more than we will get if we do nothing."

He looked back to Lewis who again nodded in agreement. Kelly shot up from his chair.

"All right, if this is how it's gonna be, let's do it right. Gather all MDF personnel here. Use no comms or trackable communication at all. Doyle. I want you to take the two guys out front. Get to the weapon stores at the airfield, and load up everything you can onto the cars and trucks there. Bring them along. We're heading for the forests south of here. They are our best chance. I want everything here within an hour. Personnel, supplies, the lot, so get to it."

* * *

Taylor awoke feeling like a new man. He had no idea how long he had been out for, and didn't care to even check on his watch. Parker had gone. It was a sign of how exhausted he must have been. She would have had to climb over him to get out, and it hadn't woken him. A shower was his first port of call, but afterwards, he realised he had but one uniform. The dirty one he had been wearing.

Walking about without the Reitech equipment was a revelation. For all the power and protection it gave, it was a true sense of freedom to be out of it. Taylor put on his pistol belt and carried on to the bridge, safe in the knowledge the ship was now free of enemy combatants.

As he approached the bridge, he heard a heated argument from the far corridor.

Not a good sign, he thought.

When such a discussion was happening in public for all to hear, he knew things were bad. He stepped aboard the bridge and could hear Huber say forcefully over an open comms channel.

"This is not your fleet, and I will not submit to your authority. Its survival is a military decision and, as such, will be made by the military leader of this fleet."

No response came.

"They have cut communications, Sir," one of the crew said.

"Shit!" Huber shouted angrily.

He looked over and saw Taylor at the entrance to the bridge.

"Ah, good. Colonel, you have had more than a few run-ins with civilian authority and made it through. Maybe you can help."

Taylor took in a deep breath and stepped forward wearily. It was the last thing he wanted to deal with.

"Admiral. Given the choice of fighting the enemy with my own hands or dealing with politicians, give me the gunfight any day."

Huber laughed.

"Sadly true. The British Deputy Prime Minister is

leading a collective of other civilian high rankers in an attempt to form a government. He's a son of a bitch called Andrew Bletchley."

"What about the President?"

Huber shook his head.

"Vice President? Joint chiefs?"

"The President's ship was destroyed well before it got out of the atmosphere, confirmed by several sources. Chief of the National Guard is with us but wounded. A few Senators made it...but not a lot else. We've lost a lot getting this far."

"Well we need a government, don't we? We have a fleet, but the majority are civilians. It's not a military fleet. It is a civilian one under the protection of the Navy."

"Yes, yes, we need a government, but they want to carry on as if nothing has happened at all. We cannot let these people rule when what we need at this time is a war leader, not a peacetime one."

Taylor opened his mouth to speak but stopped himself. He could already see they were facing the kind of infighting he had always strived to avoid, and yet rarely managed.

"Follow me," Huber said.

He led Taylor into his private quarters, took a seat, and welcomed Taylor to do the same.

"What do I do, Colonel?"

"Talk to them."

Huber laughed.

"Didn't you hear me doing that when you arrived?"

"Like it or not, you are a politician now, as well as an Admiral. You are going to have to deal with the civilians, so better to make your peace now and make it work. Ignore them or put up barriers between yourselves, and it'll only get worse."

"I only wish they would have your common sense and vision. All right, I'll meet with them, but you are coming along for the ride. Seems like there is more good you can do than just fight."

Taylor knew he did not have a choice.

* * *

"All present and accounted for, Sir," said Captain Reynolds.

The former MDF soldiers were formed up in the street outside Kelly's home. There wasn't a single uniform among them, just a rag tag mix of civilian clothing and camouflage items taken from the airfield. Half of them had weapons.

"What's the headcount?"

"Two hundred and twelve ready to fight, Sir. Three hundred and twenty eight civilians."

"There are no civilians anymore," Kelly added, "You're either a fighter or you're dead."

He climbed up onto the roof of his truck parked in front of the house.

"You all know what has happened here. Earth has fallen. Armies have fallen, and governments have fallen."

"They've left us here to die!" one of the soldiers cried out.

A few yelled in support of the man.

"No, they have just done everything in their power to make sure the human race goes on. But us? We might as well be dead already. For those that made it off this world there is hope. For us, there is only war, death, and sacrifice. Do not be under any illusions. They have come here to kill us and will succeed. So the only question remains, how do you want to die? Will you be put up against a wall and shot like cattle? Will you go into one of their death camps, or be subject to their experiments? Will you put a gun in your mouth and pull the trigger?"

Many were open mouthed in shock. Nobody said a word. They waited for the good news, as they expected there must be some.

"If one of those options is favourable to you, I suggest you do it now!" he shouted, "Where I am going is right to hell, and I am dragging every one of those sons of bitches with me that I can manage. This isn't survival. This is revenge. This is payback. Will you die as sheep, or will you die as warriors? There are no rules any longer. If you follow me now, you know there is no line I will not cross. No sacrifice I will not make. I will do anything and everything in my power to make those alien bastards pay for what they have done to us. Who's with me?"

There was silence for a moment. It was a grim prospect, and he knew it. But he also knew their hatred of the aliens was all that could fuel them any longer.

"I am!" Doyle finally answered him.

Doyle had always been a quiet and reserved young man, but this was the day he changed. This had been the day he showed Kelly the way and now stood by him for all to see. Kelly nodded in appreciation.

"We never got the payback we deserved for what they did to us on our own colony. Now is our chance!" Kelly spoke to them all.

The crowd suddenly erupted into a frenzy of excitement, shouting and whistling in support. It was utter commitment and devotion to the destruction of everything they knew and loved, and it was the only way. But as they shouted in support, a pulse smashed into the group and killed two instantly. Before they could respond, two Mech fighters soared overhead and strafed their position, causing people to scatter for cover.

"Load up and follow me!" Kelly shouted.

He jumped from the truck and went to open the driver's door when he felt a hand on his shoulder. He looked around to see Doyle.

"Sir, on me!"

It was a surprise but his newfound confidence in the man compelled him to do so. Doyle rushed over to one of the trucks he had acquired. It was a military vehicle with canvas covering on the back. He leapt up onto the rear bed, but Kelly could not understand why. As the Commander took the corner to the rear and could see inside, he understood. Doyle was fighting to pull back the canvas cover because inside was a twelve barrelled anti-aircraft gun he had taken from the airfield.

"Christ, how'd you get this thing in here?"

"Forklift truck, thought it would come in handy. Help me get this off!"

Doyle had become a different man with this new conflict, and Kelly was as surprised as he was grateful. He climbed up into the back of the vehicle, took the other side of the canvas, and started tugging it back as the fighters strafed them once again. One pulse hit the front cab of the truck and tore the roof off.

"Christ!" Kelly screamed.

With one last pull the canvas slid back, and Kelly leapt into the control seat of the gun system. He'd never used one before but had watched others do so. He hit the power button, and the engine inside fired up, giving him full control of tilt and elevation. He turned to the targeting computer. It was fizzling where a shard of metal from the front cab had embedded in it.

"Shit!"

"You'll have to fire on open sights!" Doyle yelled, "And fast, they're coming in for another run!"

Kelly turned the guns around quickly with the foot controls and took aim as the fighter came in low and opened fire. He squeezed the trigger, and all the guns burst into life in a deafening volley. The muzzle flashes blurred out most of Kelly's sight, but he could see something explode before him. The debris veered off and crashed into one of the nearby houses.

"Woohoo!" Doyle shouted, "Hell of a shot!"

Kelly could barely hear him as his eardrums were still pulsating, and he was almost deaf. They watched as the other fighter banked quickly and fled rapidly.

"You did it!" Doyle exclaimed.

Kelly got up to look around at the devastation. His house was riddled with damage, and a dozen people lay dead in the road, with several other wounded screaming in pain.

"Not soon enough," he replied.

His truck was amazingly still intact and had sustained no further damage.

Many of those who had got to ground or cover got up and looked to Kelly for orders.

"We can't stay here. The town will be crawling with Mechs within a few hours after they hear about this. Gather the wounded. Leave the dead!"

None of them wanted to hear it, but they knew it was necessary.

"Load up and let's move!"

Kelly raced towards his truck, picking up one of the wounded along the way and helping them into the back of his vehicle.

"Reynolds, you're with me!"

The two of them climbed into the front of his vehicle. They waited, watching the rest of their people embark on dozens of vehicles along the road.

"Captain, with Morris gone, you're my right hand man now, you do realise that?"

"If you will have me."

"Good man. I need to know you are with me one hundred percent. The time for compromise is over. Are you with me until the end?"

"Yes, and let it be far from now, so that we can kill as many of those fuckers as possible before our time comes."

Kelly nodded in agreement. Knowing their chance of survival was gone had given them a new resolve. They feared the enemy far less now knowing their fate was sealed.

* * *

Taylor sat around a conference table with twenty representatives of Earth, who now stood together in an attempt to create a new government. Huber had placed him at the centre, opposite them all in a crescent. He had agreed to help, but never did he expect he would be placed as a figurehead to take all the fire that would come Huber's way.

Shit, he thought.

The fresh and invigorating feeling he had awoken with was being sapped away from him as each second passed. General Dupont sat on one of the flanks with another officer he did not recognise. Huber was by Taylor's side, positioned so it appeared as though Taylor stood as his right hand.

Bletchley had led the conversation so far and barely let another person get a word in. He carried on.

"The fact remains, we must establish a workable government for us to continue operating as a society. In time we will have elections, but we need a government now. We need…"

"We get what you are saying Deputy Prime Minister," Huber interrupted, "We got it the first, second, and third time. You want to establish a civilian government then do so. But understand, that while you remain under the protection of the fleet, you will submit to the authority of the Navy. I will not have military decisions compromised by a civilian authority."

"Is that what you will have, Admiral, a military regime with a puppet civilian one? Is this the sort of democracy we fought for?"

"I'm not aware you fought for anything, Mr Bletchley."

"I played my part throughout this conflict, the same as

you."

"Sat behind a desk while my people…"

"Enough!" Dupont shouted.

The room was silenced and all looked to the Frenchman.

"We aren't making any progress here, and we're not going to if we go on. We have bigger things to worry about than this petty infighting."

"Then what do you suggest we do? We need some resolution to this before there is chaos amongst our people," replied Bletchley.

"What I suggest is irrelevant because you will not like it. And what you propose is unacceptable to those of us who have the safety of the fleet in mind."

"That is not an answer, General."

Taylor could see Dupont had to use all his willpower to refrain himself from launching a verbal assault against Bletchley, but somehow he managed it.

"Well?" Bletchley asked.

Dupont took a deep breath and finally spoke.

"Everyone around this table holds a substantial position of power. They did on Earth, and they continue to do so now. We each have concerns over our own little bit of power, whether we like it or not. None of us wants to compromise, and every one of us has some grand idea of how we should proceed. So we are at a crossroads. We need to try something different."

Nobody said a word and waited to hear the magical

solution to their problems.

"There is only one man in this room who can speak without bias or concern over his stake in a parliament or a fleet; one man who will put humanity first, and say and act without any hidden agenda. Colonel Mitch Taylor. A man I grew to hate and then love. I say we ask him to moderate, to decide what we should do. How better to act than ask a man of principle to decide for us?"

Taylor was shocked as discussions broke out through the room.

"Silence!" Huber ordered.

He got it.

"I agree with General Dupont. I have no idea what Colonel Taylor's opinions are on these matters, but I trust in his judgement. Let's hear him out. And if we can all agree with his take on this, perhaps there is a chance of getting this sorted yet, agreed?"

There was general agreement to at least hear Taylor out. Huber looked to Taylor to get started, but he didn't know where to begin. He had not planned a single word for the meeting, nor thought about anything as monumentally important as this. He coughed and cleared his throat, slowly looking around.

"I…I am not of this world, but I will give you my opinion. We are at war, and this a military fleet under wartime conditions. All decisions regarding fleet movements and activity must fall under military authority. However, the military cannot govern civilians. I thought all of this was clear to everyone. The civilians must manage and govern civilian life, while working within the framework of a military operation. These are wartime conditions, and you all have your part to play."

No one spoke as they waited for him to continue.

"We must have a civilian government for the human race, but that government must respect the knowledge and experiences of those who protect this fleet and have enabled humanity to go on. So form a government. Have military representatives within it to advise but not command the government. But activity regarding fleet management, manoeuvres, and strategy must remain within the hands of capable military leaders."

Huber looked to Bletchley, who was at least a little appeased by his proposal.

"But you will still have a Naval Admiral holding supreme power among us?" he asked.

"While you remain under the protection of the Navy, yes. When we return to Earth, or establish a colony elsewhere, that can change. But right now, you are refugees under the protection of the Navy and other armed forces. They cannot protect you to the best of their abilities unless they are able to do so in the best manner they know how."

Bletchley looked around for support, but he wasn't getting it. Most of the other representatives were happy with what they had heard.

"Finally, some progress," replied Huber, "It's as simple as this. I want a vote. A majority agreement with Taylor's proposals will see it pass, and we will jointly establish the representatives to make it happen. So now, a show of hands, all in favour."

Fifteen hands went up, and it brought a smile to Huber and a sigh of relief.

"Thank you, Gentlemen. We will resume this meeting at 0800 hours tomorrow."

Taylor was quickly out of his seat and heading for the door. Huber followed him. As they got to the corridor outside, the Admiral reached for his shoulder and stopped him dead.

"Thank you, Colonel. Thank you for standing with us."

"I didn't," he replied, "I stood for what I believe is best for us all."

CHAPTER FOUR

"First question we have to ask ourselves, and we should have dealt with this much sooner, where are we, and what the hell is the significance of this place?" Huber asked.

Taylor found himself sitting at a different table now, one with just military officials and civilian experts.

"Let me welcome Mr Reiter, who some of you have met, and all are familiar with his technology."

Reiter stepped into the room with his arm in a brace and a bandage around his forehead.

"Mr Reiter was lucky enough to make it off Earth with only minor injuries."

Taylor stepped up to Reiter and shook his good arm.

"Glad you made it, Doc. We need you."

"I know," he replied modestly.

"Okay, so I want some answers. This system we're in, what's here? Are there living inhabitants? What the hell is that gateway, and whom does it belong to? Do the Krys know of our location? What planets do we have here, what resources do they hold, and are any of them habitable to any degree? These are the questions that need answers as quickly as can be done. You have been allocated into research teams to make this happen. Get moving and do your jobs."

Taylor didn't even know what he was doing there, as he could do little to help with what they needed, but he kept his mouth shut and waited.

"Sir, I've got Admiral Huang on the line. He has requested to talk with you immediately," said one of his staff nearby.

Huber shook his head.

"All right, I'll take it in my quarters," he looked to Taylor, "Come with me."

Taylor couldn't help but feel he was being paraded around as a blunt instrument in Huber's toolbox, but there was nothing he could do about it. He followed the Admiral and took a seat opposite his desk, outside of the view of the transmission about to come through. The Chinese Admiral was displayed for Huber a few seconds later. Taylor had never seen the man before and that surprised him.

Why was he not at the meeting with Bletchley? Taylor asked himself.

"Admiral Huber. I hear you have assumed command of

this fleet and are instating a government to rule it. We have not authorised this decision, and we do not accept your self imposed position as our leader."

Here comes trouble, Taylor thought.

"As the most senior and longest serving officer of this fleet, it is both my right and duty to take the reins and see this thing through," Huber responded.

"I will not…"

Huber interrupted with a stronger tone.

"Let me make myself clear, Rear Admiral. I have seniority, and I am the leader of this fleet. Should you have a problem with that, you are most welcome to depart this fleet and go your own way. But I cannot advise more strongly against it."

Huang was speechless.

"So you will shut me and my people out? You consider that acceptable?"

"No, as a leader of your people, I fully welcome your input on all military matters, and advise you to put forward representatives for whatever government may be formed in the coming days."

"You are going to far with this, Admiral. You have not heard the last on this matter."

The transmission ended. Huber simply reached for the bottle of whisky on his desk and poured it out into two glasses before passing one to Taylor. He would never have accepted it under normal circumstances in the past, but these were not normal circumstances. He took the glass and sipped it to find it was a smooth oak flavoured vintage that sparked all his senses and brought a lovely warmth.

"Yep, when a day sucks this bad, it helps," said Huber, watching Taylor's response.

"You know I'm not a politician, Admiral?"

Huber sighed. "Son, we all have to be and do things we never wanted or expected for ourselves. You are whatever we need you to be, just as I am. You don't have to like it, you only have to give it your all."

"But I suck at it. I'm just as likely to cause as much trouble as I resolve."

"We'll see about that. You've done just fine this far."

"Huang is gonna come after you. He won't let this go."

Huber sighed. "I know, but we will deal with him in due course. We're an almost random cross section of Earth's population thrown together on a whim. We have to accept that it isn't going to be plain sailing."

Huber's communicator flashed before him, and he accepted the call.

"Sir, I have a Captain Morris requesting an audience with you."

Huber looked surprised and then to Taylor.

"He's one of mine."

"See him in," Huber replied.

The door to his quarters opened and Morris entered. Taylor could immediately see the distress in his face.

"What's up?" Taylor quickly asked before the Admiral could get a word in.

"I just heard my people didn't make it off Earth."

Huber looked to Taylor in surprise.

"You said he was one of yours?"

"He is, via the Moon Defence Force."

"Admiral, did any of my people make it?"

"I do not have that information, Captain, but I can make some enquiries."

"Please do so, Sir. They are my people. My family."

Huber got to his feet, seeing the distress in Morris' face.

"You have my word, Captain. I will do everything in my power to discover the fate of your people. They inhabited an area of Germany, if I remember correctly?"

"Yes, Sir."

"Then please leave this with me, and I will liaise with the contacts I have to find out whatever I can."

Taylor got up and went to his friend. He placed a hand on his shoulder for comfort.

"You know Kelly. He either made it out or he's fighting like hell."

"Yes, that's what worries me."

"Trust me, and trust the Admiral. We'll do what we can."

Morris accepted his promise and stepped outside the quarters. Taylor took a seat once again before the Admiral.

"This is gonna get a lot worse, you know that?" Taylor

asked.

"Yeah, I know."

"What we need more than anything else right now is to stick together, work together, and fight together. Without that we are finished."

"That's what I'm trying to do, Colonel. Just not everyone sees it that way. I think we're done here. I want you to make sure your people are on the top line and ready for anything. You defended this ship admirably. Please be ready to give such service at a moment's notice whenever we need it."

"You got it, Sir."

Taylor got up and left. He'd only been awake a few hours, and he felt like he'd endured a few days of combat. He could sense the tension throughout the ship and could only imagine how much worse it was across the rest of the fleet. As he left the Admiral's quarters, he finally looked at his watch and realised it was time to get dinner. He was hopeful he would catch a few of his unit still there.

He reached the canteen and found Parker waiting for him. There was nothing on the table before her except a glass of water. Silva sat opposite her. As he approached, they perked up. He could tell they had been waiting there for some time.

"Thought you'd vanished for good," Parker said.

"You can't get rid of me that easy."

Taylor smiled as he passed them and queued up with

a dozen others to get his meal. It was slumming it for an officer of his status, but he didn't care.

"Colonel Taylor, isn't it?" a man in the line up asked.

"Yes," Taylor replied, looking over for the source of the question. As he did so, a fist struck his jaw and snapped his neck back. He staggered back a pace before getting his footing. He looked back in surprise to see a tall, well built Captain had struck him, and his eyes were full of hate and fury, yet Taylor could not understand why. The man wore a Naval uniform, but he was not American. As he turned slightly, Taylor could see a Spanish flag on his shoulder.

Parker and Silva leapt to their feet and came to Taylor's aid, but he held up his hand to stop them in their tracks.

"That's right, you son of a bitch, about time you fought your own battles!" the Captain sneered.

"Man, who the fuck are you?"

"Captain Rodrigo Cordero."

Taylor spat out blood.

"And what the hell is your beef? You just took a cheap shot like a cheap bitch. So what is it?"

"You're a traitor, Taylor. You changed sides like the wind. You just pick and choose as suits you each day, and expect everyone to rally around you and treat you as some great fucking hero."

"He is a fucking hero, you low life asshole!" Parker shouted.

She tried to rush forward in a frenzy, but Silva took

hold of her and held her back.

"That's right. You need a woman to fight for you because you're too pussy to fight for real. Sure, you'll fight on TV. You'll fight some bullshit theatre for all your audience to applaud, but when the real fight comes, you can't handle it."

Taylor was astonished by what he was hearing. He could only imagine the man had bought into the propaganda spun by the UEN and the Krys agents working within it.

"You don't know me. You've not seen what I've seen. What gives you the right to spill this kind of crap about me? What have you done through these wars? I've bled and fought, and suffered, and endured. I won't justify myself to any one, let alone some low life sailor boy like you."

The Spaniard picked up a nearby chair and swung it at Taylor, but he caught the legs and pulled hard so that the man was launched off his feet and over onto another table. The Captain sprawled rather unceremoniously over the table and landed the far side on the deck.

"Whatever hate you've built, it's all bullshit," Taylor said, watching the man haul himself to his feet.

He could see the bitter anger was burning ever greater in the Captain's eyes. He wanted to kill, and there was no doubt about it. He rushed at Taylor in a frenzy and swung a hook with all his force. It was a powerful strike, but it was off balance and telegraphed. Taylor ducked under and delivered a sharp uppercut to his stomach, causing the man's legs to lift off the ground slightly.

Taylor did not let up. He grabbed Cordero's hair with his left hand and punched him with three heavy rights until blood gushed from his face, finally throwing him down onto the floor.

Cordero's friends went to help him to his feet, but Taylor launched towards him. As he did so, one of the man's friends swung for him, and it was all the cue Silva needed to join the affray, and Parker with him.

A few minutes' later six men lay on the deck unconscious or crying in pain. Taylor, Silva, and Parker remained standing, and the ship's marines rushed in with the master-at-arms in tow. They instantly recognised Taylor and hesitated, to which he responded.

"What are you waiting for? Do your jobs!"

Ten minutes later he found himself on a bench in the brig, with Parker and Silva in adjoining cells. After a few minutes of taking it all in Parker began to laugh. Her white teeth were coated in her own blood.

"What is so funny?" Silva asked.

"You know how good that felt? To not be fighting some giant monster, but to have a good old fashioned tussle? Makes me feel alive, more than I have done in a while."

Silva shrugged. He understood what she meant but was hesitant to agree.

"What the hell was that guy's problem?" he asked.

Finally, Taylor responded.

"He wasn't wrong. Back before all this shit went down, I did change sides, and you know it. So did a lot of people. It was civil war on Earth. Only reason he picked on me is because I was on the news, and people made a big deal about it."

"But you only ever did what you thought was right," Silva replied.

"Yeah, and look where that's gotten us."

"It's got us here alive."

Taylor sat back against the wall and sighed. He couldn't believe how many times he had been behind bars now, and somehow, he knew it was far from the last time. He knew the only way he could ever break the cycle was to become top brass, and that was the last thing he ever wanted to do.

"You're still an asshole!"

It was Cordero. He recognised the voice. He looked past the bars of his cell and across to the opposite cell. The shadowy figure had been there since they arrived, and it had not occurred to him that's who it would be.

"You wouldn't even be here if it wasn't for him!" Parker called out in his defence.

No response came, but Taylor already knew the man would be more trouble. They could hear the door to the brig open and footsteps approaching. There were more than two sets of footsteps, and that meant someone of note was coming, but Taylor made no attempt to get up.

A few seconds later, Huber stepped into view; he was surrounded by marines. He stopped at Taylor's cell and simply stared at him.

"This asshole came looking for trouble, Admiral. He is a danger to this fleet!" Cordero screamed.

"Shut up, Captain!"

Huber turned to him.

"You are assigned to this ship, but I am still your superior officer, just as Colonel Taylor is!"

He turned back to Taylor.

"Really?" he asked, "All the shit we have to deal with, and you brawl with idiots like him? You have to get yourself together, Colonel. I need you. The people need you. But they need Colonel Taylor, saviour of humanity. The same Taylor who defeated Demiran, not the mess I am seeing here now. Earlier today, I thought you had come through for us and you had, and now I have to deal with this? What do you have to say for yourself?"

Taylor said nothing.

"Right now I need you. I need all of you," Huber continued, "So you keep whatever this is bottled up, never to come out. Not until we are back home on Earth, and all of this is over. I don't care what it was about or why it started, that's the deal. You all got that?"

"Yes, Sir," they all said in tune, except Taylor who remained silent.

"Goddamn it, Taylor, are you with us or not?"

Taylor shook his head.

"In all these years, why do people keep asking me that?"

"Probably because you keep getting into this shit. I don't need a troublemaker, Taylor. I need the legend that is Colonel Mitch Taylor. Can you be that man? Because that is the man, that is the marine these people need. So are you gonna be that man?"

Taylor looked across to Parker and could see she was nodding for him to agree. Not just to get them out of the mess they were in, but because she genuinely believed in the Admiral's words. He looked back to Huber.

"You have my word I will do everything I can to get us back home and to win."

Huber sighed. "Good enough. Get this lot out of here!"

The cell doors opened, and Huber was waiting for Taylor.

"You're coming with me."

Taylor knew he had no choice in the matter, but he accepted his sidearm and carried on beside the Admiral.

When they were clear of the brig, Huber finally opened up the real reason he was released so soon.

"Colonel, we've got problems. Problems we could both see coming, and I need your help.

"What is it now?"

"Dissent among the fleet. Huang is winning support amongst a number of the ships. People are starting to question who should be in command, and what we should be doing. Some want to return to Earth and think we should never have left. Others want to see a President elected to rule us. It's a goddamn disaster."

"I told you, Sir, I am not a politician."

"Yes you are, Colonel. You have been for a long time, whether you like it or not. Look, Taylor, there are many things in life we have to deal with that we don't like and don't want to do. You just want to lead marines and fight the good fight; I get it. But the people need more from you than that because you are capable of more."

"Not sure I agree, Admiral, but I can't hide the fact I am glad to be out. What is it you actually want me to do?"

"Huang, he is the key to this. He has some sway over the fleet, particularly those from the far eastern nations, but his support is growing. Huang is a good officer and a good Admiral, but he has no idea what to do in this situation of ours. He is going to get a lot of folk killed unless he can be made to see straight."

Taylor was sick to death of being forced into verbal onslaughts to convince people he had no care for, but he knew he had no choice.

"How on Earth am I supposed to convince a Chinese Admiral to accept your authority?" he asked.

"I don't know, but that's your task now, and I have every faith in you."

Taylor was led towards the bridge by Huber but stopped short where he found his Reitech suit awaiting him.

"Expecting trouble?"

"I want you to convey the image of Taylor the marine. I need you to both intimidate and bring a sense of confidence in us all at the same time."

Taylor pulled on his gear and carried on to the bridge where all the crew there turned to him, as if he would be able to speak some magical words that would end all their troubles. Admiral Huang was projected on a screen before him for all to see and hear.

"This is Colonel Taylor. He will act as mediator for us."

Mediator? That isn't how it was sold to me.

But he could see from Huang's response to his presence that his reputation went a long way.

"It is an honour, Colonel Taylor. I am so glad you made it here to fight with us."

"I didn't come here to fight," replied Taylor, "We came here to survive. Maybe that involves fighting, maybe not. All that matters is the human race survives, and for that we need to stick together and work together."

Huang did not reply.

"If that is to be the case, this fleet needs a leader."

"But it should not be Admiral Huber, the leader of the failed operation in enemy space."

"Oh, really? And who should it be, someone with no experience that any of us have heard of? You? You have a third the vessels the US Navy has in this fleet. And you think you should be in charge? Huber is the obvious choice for this. Accept him, or leave this fleet and do not come back!"

The transmission cut off.

"What the hell was that?" Huber asked.

"You asked me to negotiate. Well, this is how I do it."

"Are you trying to pick a fight, Colonel?"

Taylor turned to him and responded angrily.

"I am doing what you asked me to in the best way I know how. If you don't like it, then why did you spring me from that cell? I will be a puppet to no one. I have been there, and I didn't like it the first time."

"Sir, the Chinese Battleship Lo Yang is launching fighters."

"Power up weapons, launch fighters," replied Huber.

He turned to Taylor.

"What have you done?"

"This shitstorm was coming whether we wanted it or not. Let's get it over with now before we really are deep in the shit."

"That was not your decision to make, Colonel."

"You put me in this position, Sir. I never wanted it."

"You see, Sir. Can you see him for the troublemaker he is?"

Taylor looked around to see Cordero standing on the bridge behind him.

"What the hell is he doing here, Admiral?"

"Captain Cordero is here to represent the interests of

the Spanish Navy and her South American allies, who make up more than a sizeable amount of this fleet."

Taylor could see the smug look in Cordero's face, but he did not care for it.

"Sir, fighters are ready to launch," said Vega.

"I said launch, not prepare to launch. Get them out there!"

Taylor could see everyone on the bridge was uneasy with their position.

"Sir..." said Lieutenant Capwell.

"What is it?" he replied impatiently.

"Sir, A number of ships are moving out of formation and heading for the Lo Yang."

"What are their intentions?"

"Admiral Huang will not accept your authority," stated Cordero.

Taylor and Huber turned, suddenly realising the Spaniard knew more than he was letting on.

"All right, I'll indulge you. Speak," replied Huber.

"I am here to represent my people, who like Admiral Huang, are concerned about the direction you are taking this fleet in."

"Direction? We haven't even got a direction. We just got here."

"There are many concerned parties that do not believe you are the right man for the job, Admiral. Your track record thus far is far from exemplary."

Taylor knew he referred to their disastrous incursion into enemy territory, but that was not a fair blow to strike. General Dupont strode aboard the bridge in the silence that ensued.

"What the hell is going on?" he demanded.

Taylor leaned over to him and responded quietly.

"We've got trouble. Admiral Huang is trying to seize power, and he's got a fair amount of support."

Dupont shook his head. "Huang? He's a crazy fool."

"A fool with a wealth of resources, though."

"Sir, we've got a signal coming in from the Lo Yang," said Vega.

"Put it through."

Huang appeared before them. He was a young Admiral with boyish looks, and although he must be at least thirty, he didn't look it. Huber opened his mouth to speak but was interrupted by Huang.

"Admiral Huber. You have been unwilling to hear and act upon the concerns of myself and many other Captains in this fleet. We therefore have no choice but to demand you stand down as Admiral of this fleet, a position that was never awarded to you, nor were you entitled to bestow upon yourself. We insist that you step down and accept negotiations as to the structure of this fleet. Or.."

"Or what? You'll fire on us? You'll fire on what remains of the human race? You wouldn't be here if it weren't for us and this ship, and don't you forget it!"

He cut off the transmission and looked to Capwell.

"Open a channel to the fleet."

"Everyone, Sir?"

"Yes, absolutely everyone, including the Lo Yang. I want everyone to hear this."

"Yes, Sir."

Capwell nodded to the Admiral to acknowledge he was now live with the entire fleet.

"This is the Admiral speaking. Admiral Huber of the Washington, flagship of the fleet. The Washington is the most powerful vessel we have, and as the highest ranked senior Naval officer, the responsibility of this fleet falls into my hands. I did not ask for this nor seek it. I don't want to rule as a President nor King. I will continue to serve in the capacity I always have done. But there are others among us who would seek to divide our forces and struggle for power themselves."

He looked to Taylor for support. Taylor nodded in agreement, and he went on.

"The survival of the fleet is dependent on us sticking together and doing what is best for us all. I will not tolerate dissent among the officers. It is a luxury we cannot afford. In time, we will establish a civilian government, and that process is already underway. But I want to assure you all, that I will do everything in my power to protect this fleet. Admiral Huang is taking up arms against us and is therefore threatening our safety. Those who would follow him and recklessly endanger all we have fought to defend, go now. Go, or stay and submit to my command."

He looked to Dupont who stood beside him in support.

"Admiral Huang, you have five minutes to recall your fighters and stand down. You may either end this peacefully so that we may go about our lives, or leave the fleet. The alternative will be your destruction."

Huber ended the transmission and watched the map projected on the table before them. He could see three warships embark for Huang's position, and one came back over to theirs.

"This will not end well."

"No, Colonel Taylor," he replied, "but I didn't pick this fight, and I'll be damned if I am going to back down and be walked over by this son of a bitch. What else could I have done?"

Taylor had no idea how to respond to that.

"I didn't say I had all the answers, but this isn't what we need right now."

"It wasn't of my choosing. If Huang wants to pick a fight, then that's his choice, but we'll be the ones to end it. Order all civilian craft to fall back twenty klicks to this point," said Huber as he pointed to the map.

"Anyone here know Huang? Anyone know what sort of man he is?"

"I do."

They looked around to see it was Cordero who had

spoken.

"Will he fire on us? Is he that crazy?"

"He will do whatever is necessary to ensure the best course of action for this fleet."

"If he's as power hungry as he sounds, I have no doubt he will fire," Taylor added.

"Power hungry? That is rather rich coming from you all. You have seized power and have the audacity to call those who question it troublemakers. And you, Taylor, your loyalties turn like the wind. You are not a man to be trusted."

"Sir, I have Admiral Huang for you," said Capwell.

"Put him through!" Huber bawled.

"Admiral, stand down!" Huber pleaded with him.

"I am sorry but I cannot. If I allow you to continue on this path, it sets a dangerous precedent. If the fleet and her leaders agree to accept you as their leader, then I will stand by it, but they have not. You must stand down and bow to the will of your peers."

"I bow to nobody's will."

"Sir, Lo Yang fighters are in range of ours," Capwell interrupted.

"Don't be a fool, Huang. We cannot afford to lose lives over a petty dispute."

"There is nothing petty about this. We are fighting for the good of us all."

As he finished, Cordero quickly drew his sidearm and

rushed towards Huber.

"Admiral Huber, I am placing you under arrest!"

Taylor had seen it happen out of the corner of his eye, and as the Spaniard approached the Admiral, he launched forward. With one hand he took hold of Cordero's pistol, and the other struck him full force with a straight punch to the head. Taylor forgot his strength afforded by the Reitech suit, and the impact snapped Cordero's neck. He became limp and collapsed onto the deck of the bridge. Taylor was appalled his own savagery and was speechless. He looked around to see that nobody made a single move, but Huang had seen it all on the video feed.

"Admiral Huber. Can you not see your failings? If this is how you run your ship, what hope is there for the fleet? I must insist you arrest Colonel Taylor immediately and stand down from your command."

Huber looked to Taylor and could see the sadness in his eyes, but he was appreciative, knowing what the Colonel had done for him. He looked back to Huang with disgust.

"You did this. You caused this young man, this young officer to die. His death is on your hands, as will many others today. I have never done anything to endanger the people under my command unnecessarily. I will not fire first, but know that if you do, you will be finished. I will ensure your death or imprisonment. This fleet will go on, and it will survive, but not while people like you meddle with power."

"Sir, I have B squadron commander asking for orders. They are closing fast with Lo Yang fighters," said Vega.

Huber looked back to Huang for an answer, but he said nothing.

"Order the Commander to not fire unless fired upon."

He had not taken his eyes off of Huang.

"I am sorry we could not resolve this peacefully, Admiral."

"Sir, I'm getting a massive energy signature five klicks off the port side," said Capwell.

"What the hell is it?" Huber asked.

He looked back to Huang.

"What have you done?"

Huang looked confused. "We are reading the same signature, but it is not of our doing."

"What the hell is going on?" Huber shouted.

He rushed over Capwell's console. The man seemed fixated on it. Taylor snapped out of his daze and raced to the Admiral's side.

"What is that?" the Admiral asked.

They were looking at what appeared to be some form of ship. It had a sleek slim profile and engines self-contained within the structure. The skin of the vessel partly mimicked the space around it and blended in well enough they had to look hard to identify it as a ship at all. It reminded Taylor of some of the stealth technology used by Karadag's forces in the first war.

"Huang, are you seeing this?" Huber shouted.

"Yes, whatever it is."

"Alert all fighters, redeploy to form a wall between us and this vessel, but do not approach behind two klicks of it."

He heard Huang issue similar orders.

"Jafar, get your ass over here!" Taylor called out.

The alien quickly came to their side and looked at the screen with the same puzzling expression as they had.

"What is it? Where did it come from?"

"Admiral, I have no idea," replied Capwell.

"Sir," added Vega, "unknown vessel is powering up."

"Weapons?"

"No idea."

"Get a firing solution on whatever it is and await my orders. And get that thing displayed on the ops table so we can get a better look!"

As the screen projected before them, lights began to glow on the craft and encased it in two bands of blue light.

"I don't like this," Taylor said.

"Prepare to fire," Huber ordered.

A dazzling flashed erupted around the unknown ship, forcing them all to look away for a second, and then look back to see it was gone.

"Where the hell is it?"

"Sir, it looks like it created its own space gateway and jumped out."

Taylor shook his head. "We are not alone. This will not end well."

CHAPTER FIVE

"I want to know what that ship is, where it came from, and where it's gone!" yelled Huber.

"Sir, Squadron Commander Hunter is requesting orders."

"He turned around to see Huang was still displayed before him and waiting to see his response.

"Admiral, can we at least agree to cease all hostilities while potentially greater threats remain?"

"Agreed, but this is not over."

The transmission cut off.

"Call our fighters back, and get the civilian fleet back here under our protection."

He looked to all the officers and experts around him. Finally, he glared at Jafar.

"It's about time you came clean about all this. What the hell was that ship? Start talking!"

"I have never seen it before," he replied calmly.

"Never seen it before? Christ! You took us to this place, and you had no idea what it was and what was here?"

"It was the only place I knew there would not be a Krys colony or outpost."

"So what the hell was that ship we just saw?"

"Not Krys."

Huber shook his head. He wanted to carry on but knew he wasn't getting anywhere.

"Does anybody have any goddamn answers for me?"

"Sir, I'm getting an emergency distress signal from the Goeben."

"Put it through."

"It's an automated signal, Sir."

"Hail her Captain, and find out what the hell is going on."

"I'm trying, Sir, but they are not responding."

"What is their current location?"

A second later a live map projected onto Huber's operations table. The Goeben was moving at full speed towards the civilian fleet.

"What the hell are they doing?" Huber asked, "Try them again!"

Vega tried to hail them, and this time they could all hear the tension rise as his voice became louder and more concerned.

"Sir, they're not slowing down," said Capwell.

"Launch fighters and bring us within firing range."

Capwell looked surprised. "Sir, she's one of ours?"

"We don't know that for certain."

"Sir, I've got a signal coming through. It's faint and on a personal channel."

"Put it through."

"This is flight ...enant Chapman. We have been overrun by .... Goeben is compromised...peat...Goeben compromised..."

"This is Admiral Huber speaking. Who is in control of the Goeben?"

"The...troops, Mechs...ones...they're everywhere."

"Hold on, Lieutenant. We are coming for you."

"They're...find me...coming."

The bridge was silent as they heard Mech weapons fire, and the Lieutenant screamed in pain before he was finally silenced, and the comms channel ended.

"Lieutenant Chapman, come in? Lieutenant..." Capwell repeated.

"He's gone," said Huber solemnly, "Are we in weapons range yet?"

"No, Sir, at the rate she's moving, we won't catch her before she reaches the fleet."

"How long have we got?"

"She'll be on top of them in less than a minute."

"Give orders to our fighters. Take down the Goeben."

Vega relayed the commands quickly, and they could see

on their displays as light flashed in the distance, and the fighters strafed the ship.

"Sir, Goeben weapon systems are going live," said Vega.

"Tell Hunter to do whatever he has to do destroy that ship!"

"They can barely scratch it," Taylor muttered.

The weapon batteries on the Goeben opened fire, and two of their fighters were blown apart in the opening salvo as the others banked hard to avoid the incoming fire.

"Washington, we cannot penetrate the armour. We haven't got anything that'll even scratch the surface."

"Take out her engines, anything you can do!" Vega replied.

Huber turned to Capwell.

"Order the civilian fleet to scatter. I want at least two klicks between every vessel!"

They knew it was all too late, but they had to try. Gunfire struck across the engines but seemed to do little. A moment later one of the fighters put soared towards one of the engines in a suicidal attempt to ram them. The ship ignited on impact and seemingly caused one of the engines to falter for just a moment, but it was soon firing bright once more.

A moment later their weapon systems turned on the fleet, and the crew of the Washington watched helplessly as one of the barges was bombarded with shot after shot.

"How long until we have a firing solution?" Huber

asked.

"Two minutes, Sir."

"Is there no one closer?"

"Sir, the Lo Yang is closing on the Goeben and going weapons hot."

"Huang, you son of a bitch, you got there," said Huber.

The Chinese warship's bombardment was fierce, and they watched as the hull of the Goeben was smashed with everything they had.

"They're not responding to the fire. They just keep hitting the barge," Capwell said in disbelief.

"They're hitting where they know they can do the most damage," said Taylor.

Huber nodded in agreement.

Thirty seconds of continuous barrage finally brought an end to the Goeben's weapon systems, but the Lo Yang didn't let up.

Huber took a deep breath and sighed in relief as he thought they were over the worst of it. He looked to the barge and could see holes over several levels of the hull and debris where people and equipment had been sucked out.

"They're still heading for the barge, Sir."

Huber looked back to his operations table and could see the Goeben approaching the barge at great speed. The Lo Yang's weapons continued to pour fire into the vessel, but its thick hull seemed to hold, despite chunks of metal being ripped off and leaving a trail of debris.

"It's too late," said Jafar.

Huber turned around, surprised that the alien had finally offered some information without prompting.

"What do you mean?"

"They are doing the only thing they can do. They will destroy the barge and all inside in any way they can."

"They're going to ram the barge," Taylor added.

Huber snapped back around.

"Tell them to put all power to engines, and get the hell out of there now!"

"They're already at full power, Sir."

"Shit, get me Admiral Huang, now!"

"He was projected before them within seconds.

"Admiral, the Goeben intends to ram the barge."

"The Goeben has now passed beyond the safe distance we can fire at, but I am already deploying marine forces to board the vessel and protect the civilians."

"But, Admiral..."

"Huang out," he cut in.

They all watched in horror as the Goeben crashed into the hull of the barge, but to their amazement it did not penetrate fully. A hole was torn several metres wide before the nose of the Goeben began to slide down the length of the massive vessel and crash in beside it, so that the two vessels now lay in parallel and were wedged together.

The Goeben was a quarter the size of the barge, but

they all knew too well that only civilian authorities and police protected the space within the barges.

"Get me the Captain of that vessel!"

"Captain Dokgo, most of the people aboard are Korean," said Vega.

A moment later a frantic Korean man, who appeared to be in his fifties, appeared before him.

"Admiral, I have reports that alien robots have boarded this ship. What is going on?"

"Captain, you are under attack by hidden enemy elements within this fleet that have captured one of our vessels and boarded yours. We are doing everything in our power to protect you."

Screams could be heard over the comms channel.

"They're here. They're killing everyone. There are dozens of them, maybe hundreds... Admiral, please don't leave us!"

"I won't leave you, Captain. We already have marines en route to help. Are you in a safe area?"

"The bridge is safe, yes."

"If you have blast doors, seal them."

"But all those people?"

"Captain, just listen to me. Close your blast doors. Lock down the bridge."

"Yes, yes, okay."

Now, do you still have power to your engines?"

"Yes...yes we do."

"We are sending you coordinates now, reposition and await assistance."

"But, Admiral, I am watching people die now. They're being slaughtered. How…"

"Captain Dokgo, listen to me. Redirect the coordinates we are sending you. We are doing everything we can to help you. Now I have to get to work. Stay on this line. I am passing you onto my number two…"

Vega took over the conversation on his own handset.

"Huang's marines, what chance do they have?"

"We have no idea of the enemy strength or firepower."

"What are their chances?"

"It's a big ship and a lot of civilians to get in the way."

"What are their chances?" Huber yelled.

Taylor shook his head. "If his marines are equipped and experienced anything like the marines you had aboard the Washington when I got here, not great."

Huber shook his head and began to pace up and down the ship.

"We've got twenty thousand people on that ship. God knows how many are already dead. And now you're telling me the rescue operation is destined to fail? I will not lose those people. We can't afford such losses! Taylor, how quickly can you get your people together for a full breach of the barge?"

"Admiral. Our Mastiffs are beaten to hell. We have one fully operational at best. You haven't got enough transports to get us over there in any great number, and we haven't got enough in my unit alone to get this done right."

"You? You of all people can't get this done?"

"Right now it's about saving as many lives as possible. I can go in there, and sure we'll kill every last one of those bastards in time, but not quick enough. We need a rapid response, and we need it now. We need the weight of numbers now. In short, we gotta get there firstest with the mostest, and we're already failing on one of those things."

'Time is short Taylor. Tell me what you need, and I'll do it."

"Crank this boat up, get us over there, and dock with that barge. Arm everyone you can with a weapon and send us aboard en masse."

Huber was shocked.

"Dock? When Mechs run amok?"

"It's all or nothing, Admiral. We can go in with maybe sixty marines now, and everyone aboard that ship could be dead before we have the job done, or we can go in en mass. I have close to three hundred marines at my disposal, and you yourself can spare a couple of hundred. Find Major Moye and have him deploy anything he can at the same time. Admiral, we can be hitting back within ten minutes, or we can piss about and lose a shitload of lives."

Huber did not reply. He was stunned by the situation.

"Don't risk it, Sir!" Vega pleaded, "We cannot risk the ship for the lives of a few civilians!"

"A few civilians!" Huber repeated in desperation.

He turned back to Taylor.

"Get your people ready and make sure this works," He looked back to Vega, "Do it."

Vega shook his head at the order, but he did not dare defy it. Taylor raised his arm and opened a channel on his comms unit.

"Inter-Allied, gather your gear and prepare for immediate assault."

"How long until we reach their location?"

"I can have us alongside in two minutes and docked a short while after that, Admiral."

"Short while?" Taylor asked, "People are dying in there, probably in great numbers, get in there now!"

He waited for someone to order the ship's Marine detachment into operation, but it did not come.

"Admiral. I need every one of your marines prepped and ready to board that barge with us. Have everyone who isn't currently working a vital job to grab a rifle. You'll have to defend the access points once we get aboard by yourself."

Huber hesitantly put out the order.

"How many points of access will we have?"

Huber looked to Vega because he did not know.

"I believe we have three docking corridors that will align with the lower hull of the barges."

"Get me a layout."

On the project before him, Taylor could see the access points were almost equidistant along the length of the Washington, a ship that was only a little over half the size of the vast barges.

"For the length of this operation, these will be designated zones A, B, C, and D, Alpha, Bravo, Charlie, Delta," he said, as he went from fore to aft and finally the landing bay, "Have your marines ready the forward and middle locations at A and B. My people will take C and D."

"And Captain Moye's?"

"I don't care, just get him in there fast. We haven't got time for any great strategy here. This is a search and destroy mission, with time being a priority. How long until we dock?"

"Sixty seconds, Sir."

"You know what to do."

With that, Taylor rushed to the door and found Parker waiting for him with a gun and spare shield for his use. Jafar was there also.

"We got places to be. Let's move!"

He relayed his orders as he ran.

"Captain King, you're on."

When they reached the fighter bays, they heard a message over the comms, "Docking in three, two one.."

They felt the ship rock just a little as they clamped onto the barge. Rains was already waiting for them with another Mercury.

"Not had time to name her yet, Colonel, what do you think?"

Taylor did not stop as he strode towards the craft.

"I think we need to get a shift on. Let's go, go, go!"

Eddie could see the urgency in his face and rushed aboard. The engines were already running as Parker's platoon rushed on board after Taylor. As the door slammed shut, he got a signal through from King.

"We've got the green light. Ready on your mark."

"This is Colonel Taylor to all units. Breach, breach, breach!"

He wanted to be in there first, but he knew they couldn't wait.

* * *

"Do you know where you are going or are you hoping for the best?" Reynolds asked.

Kelly had been driving for over an hour now, without giving any indication as to his intentions or destination. They were driving at high speed along a narrow old country road, surrounded by thirty-metre high trees that at least kept them concealed from any aircraft.

"I know of a place. A system of underground bunkers deep in the heart of the forest."

"How do you know of their existence?"

"I was briefed on their presence when we first relocated

here. They're our best chance. We might even find a few allies there."

"I sure hope so."

"Don't hope, Captain. Hope didn't get us this far."

They both spotted a smoke trail rising from trees up ahead, but Kelly did not slow down.

"What do you want to do?"

"What we are already doing. Whatever may be ahead, it can't be any more danger to us than what will soon be at our backs."

Reynolds nodded in agreement. He lowered his window, raised his rifle to the frame, and took a deep breath.

"You know we'll need a lot more heavy gear than this if we're gonna make a difference."

"Got that right."

They took the bend up ahead and saw the wreck of an armoured vehicle burning on the roadside. They could already see from a distance that it was of human origin.

"Not good, not good at all. I don't like this, Boss," said Reynolds.

Kelly said nothing and continued on. As they neared the vehicle, they could see smoke arising from a few trees nearby and the tail end of a Mech fighter embedded in the foliage. That at least brought a smile to Kelly's face.

"Looks like they didn't go down without a fight."

The presence of the enemy fighter put Reynolds on edge, and he held his finger close to the trigger as they reached the wreckage. There was no sign of life by the armoured vehicles, but when they got the other side of it, they saw metal strewn across the road. Kelly stopped and got out.

"What is it?" Reynolds asked.

"Not sure."

Kelly took up his rifle and headed forwards carefully and cautiously. He studied every element of their surroundings while closing the distance, and finally recognised what he was looking at. The twisted metal shrapnel was in fact the remains of three or more Mech warriors who had been blown apart.

"Must have hit 'em with some pretty heavy ordnance," said Kelly.

"Like what?"

Kelly looked up at the large bore barrel of the wrecked vehicle beside them.

"Another one of those, I guess."

"So there were survivors here?"

Kelly let out a deep breath.

"I'd say so," he said, looking at the tank tracks continuing on past the wreckage.

"You see, hope," said Reynolds.

Kelly looked over to the wreck of the fighter and moved towards it.

"Sir, shouldn't we keep moving?"

"Not if there's any chance of some bastard alive in that

thing. We've kept our movements quiet till now. Let's be sure to leave no stragglers like we did back in town."

He moved up cautiously through the foliage with his weapon held at the ready. As he neared the ship, he stopped dead on seeing two bodies ahead. They were both Mechs. He looked around for any sign of movement, but there was nothing. He carried on until he reached them and soon realised they were riddled with bullets from human made guns.

"Looks like they were hit wholesale, fish in a barrel," added Reynolds.

"Good."

"Whoever came through here meant business."

"Sounds like our kind of people, Reynolds."

"Yeah...maybe." He stepped nearer and could see just how much fire had been poured into the two Mechs. Someone had really gone to town on them.

"All right, let's move."

They got back on the road and navigated their way past the debris and carried on through the seemingly endless forest.

"You really know where you're going, Sir?"

"Have I ever bullshitted you, Captain?"

"No, Sir."

"Have I ever made anything up?"

"No, Sir."

"Have I ever led you into a trap?"

"No, Sir...but.."

"But nothing. Either say something useful or interesting, or shut the hell up."

Reynolds was silenced. He could tell Kelly had become a new man. He had reverted to the cold hard calculating warrior he had been when they were fighting for survival on the Moon. Kelly knew it, too, but he didn't mind. He knew he had to be an entirely different kind of animal to make a difference now.

They carried on for another ten kilometres when Reynolds could hardly contain himself any longer.

"How much farther until we reach the complex?"

Kelly turned and glared at him.

"You want me to be your number two, start treating me like it. I need to know our operational plans. I need to know locations. Whatever you know or plan, I need to know it, too."

Kelly nodded.

"Good, now you're starting to think like a leader."

"Don't ask what you need to know, demand it."

"Got it."

"Then we are two klicks away from the first of the bunkers. They are not written down. They are on no map. Their location was on a need-to-know basis. I needed to know, and now you do, too. I do not have coordinates for their location. They are not near any town or settlement I know of. I only know how to reach them by memory, and you must do the same. That tank, the bodies, the fighter. Those are gonna have to go once we are set up. They are identifying landmarks, and that is something to be avoided."

Kelly suddenly brought the vehicle to a standstill. Reynolds looked ahead at a large fallen tree ahead. It was completely cutting off access to the road.

"You don't stop for a smouldering tank, but you stop for a fallen tree?"

"It's too convenient. The vehicle back there was purposely moved out of the way for access."

"Okay?"

"And so if whoever it was came this way, they'd have to have moved that tree, or they purposely placed it there."

"Or it could just be a fallen tree?"

Kelly turned to Reynolds who he could hear wasn't taking it seriously.

"Here's a philosophy to live by. Treat every coincidence like a kill zone."

"You just made that up, didn't you?"

"Damn right I did, because you needed to hear it."

"All right, so is it a barrier or a trap? I don't see what we can do about it, anyway."

"Go tell the vehicles behind. I want a dozen shooters on each flank to work their way through the trees, and have a few extra guys jump on the back of my truck."

"Got it."

"And, Captain…you make sure they're well armed!"

"Yes, Sir."

A few minutes later they were rolling forward along the trail at a walking pace to match those going through cover to their flanks. They had left the rest of the convoy behind. Kelly knew all too well what a death trap a narrow road could be, but he didn't regret taking it. Reynolds hung onto the side of the truck, ready to leap off at a moment's notice.

The road was so quiet; Kelly could hear the sounds of twigs breaking in the wooded areas as they advanced. He drove with one hand on the wheel and a rifle in the other.

"Would the Krys set a trap like this?" Reynolds asked, "Seems a bit subtle for them."

"I doubt it, but we've been surprised too many times by the things they have done. We have to assume they are capable of anything."

They were just twenty metres away from the fallen tree now, and had neither seen nor heard anything amiss. Kelly looked around frantically, desperately trying to spot the first sign of trouble. Finally, he rocked up in front of the tree and brought the vehicle to a halt. As he did so, he spotted something in the distance. He squinted to identify what he was seeing, finally recognising a wide bore cannon barrel protruding from dense foliage less than thirty metres beyond the tree.

"Gun! Get down!"

"He jumped out from his truck and took a knee beside it, but as he did so, he heard a wave of shouts of screams up ahead.

"Put your weapons down! Stand down!" they called.

"They're human. We're okay," Reynolds said.

He began to get up when Kelly shouted at him.

"Get your ass down!"

"Identify yourselves!" a voice called. He peered through the branches of the fallen tree but could still not identify any people.

"Commander Kelly, formerly of the MDF!"

No response came for while until finally…

"The what?"

"Moon Defence Force!" Reynolds shouted.

"Sir, they're friendlies," he added.

"We don't know that."

"Was it you shot down that Krys fighter back there?" Kelly shouted.

"Affirmative!"

Kelly got to his feet and clambered over the tree, carrying on in the open for all to see clearly. He held is rifle low but did not drop it, and held is other hand up to show he was no threat.

"Put your weapons down!" a voice ordered.

He was starting to pinpoint the location now by sound but could still not see it.

"Put 'em down!"

He stopped in his tracks and stood calmly head on towards where the voice was coming from, a few metres to the right of the gun barrel.

"If you are fighting the Krys, then we are allies."

"Put your weapon down!"

"And I put my weapon down for no man nor alien!" Kelly bellowed in return.

They all waited for a response. Reynolds looked around cautiously from the cover of Kelly's truck, but he could still see nothing.

"Did you hear me?" Kelly asked, "Shoot me, or come out!"

Kelly still made no attempt to neither raise his rifle nor move.

"Ball's in your court!"

Finally, he saw a few branches shake, and part of the tree seemed to get up and walk into the road. A man wearing a camouflage ghillie suit made of part man made materials and part local foliage stood before him. The man was so padded out and bulky he looked like a gorilla. Kelly said nothing and waited for the man to pull back his hood and reveal his face. As they did so, Kelly was shocked to see it was a woman inside.

A woman as tall as he was with her hair tied back and a both curious and suspicious look on her face. Her voice was so deep, and her body so tall and strong, it was hard to notice she was a woman.

"Corporal Berlin, of the…well not sure anymore. We have no unit. We are on our own."

"Commander Kelly, formerly of the MDF."

"You can't carry on this way, Commander."

"I'm not a Commander anymore. Call me Kelly."

She looked back past the tree to the line of vehicles in the distance.

"Still look like a Commander to me," she replied, "I am sorry, but I cannot allow you to pass. Turn your vehicles and go back the way you came."

Kelly shook his head.

"Guessing you got a few friends back there."

She did not respond.

"And I am guessing if you were asked by a stranger to walk to your death, you'd not agree and start walking? No… not a chance."

He could see she was starting to understand, but she had strict orders, and she was sticking to them.

"No, you wouldn't do it, would you? I have a few hundred people here, and every one of them a fighter. So here's the deal. We either keep going the way we are going, or you fire on us."

She shook her head.

"I cannot allow you to continue, Commander."

Taylor began to walk forward. As he did so, he let go of the rifle slung at his side and held both hands up as to not appear any threat. He walked cautiously and carefully towards the woman whose rifle was now carefully trained on him.

"Whoever you are, you want to fight the bastards who have invaded this world. We do, too. We aren't running from a fight. We're regrouping and establishing a guerrilla movement. However many people you have, honestly tell me you can't use more?"

He kept creeping forwards and was now just a few metres from the woman. Because of her ghillie suit, he could see no insignia or rank. Her accent was German, but that was hardly a surprise.

"Stop right there, or I'll shoot!" she yelled.

He kept moving forward.

"I won't. I can't, just as you can't shoot me. We're the same. We want the same thing, and we're in this together," replied Kelly.

He finally reached the barrel of her gun.

"Whoever you are, put it down, and let's do this together. I'm not here through any accident. I know the location of the bunkers in these forests. I was briefed when I was relocated here. All I want is a chance to fight these things. I know you want the same. Don't make us fight each other now. We're at the end of days. All we have left is our will and our raw determination to go on fighting and killing those things."

He took one step closer so that the barrel of the gun pressed against his chest.

"Let us do the only thing we have left to do in this world. We don't want your sympathy; we don't want your charity. We're fighters. Let us fight."

The woman was shocked and frozen as she clung to her rifle. She was clearly a hardened veteran and a tough soldier, but she came close to tears as she began to quiver a little. She turned back to the trees where she knew her people were.

"Lower you're weapons. These are friendlies!"

A number of the trees rustled, and three more soldiers stepped out into the open.

"Corporal Berlin of the… I don't even know anymore, Commander."

"Kelly."

"Commander Kelly."

"Just Kelly. Maybe I was a Commander one day past. Times change, we change."

She nodded in agreement and looked back to her people. "Clear the way, let them through!"

A few trees around the gun barrel were pulled back to reveal a heavy tank carefully concealed within. They connected up a winch on the vehicle to the fallen tree and hauled it out the way in seconds.

"Pull on forwards, give enough space that all your people can get through. Then wait for me. You'll need me with you to avoid this down the road."

"Thank you."

"Don't thank me, I'm just the first line of defence. You'll have to convince my superiors yet."

Kelly strode back to his vehicle and waved on for the other vehicles to join them. Reynolds stepped into the vehicle as he did, sighing a great sigh of relief as he sat down.

"How did you know she wouldn't fire?"

"If they didn't, there was no hope to this anyway," replied Kelly.

"Hope? You told me…"

"Yeah, I tell you what you need to hear, Captain. Be it a lesson for you, sometimes those you are responsible for need you to say or do certain things. It isn't always easy, but it's the price of command."

"And if I didn't want command at this level?"

"Hard luck and tough shit."

CHAPTER SIX

"I'm getting reports of some serious shit going down!" Rains shouted out.

Their craft passed through the landing bay doors only to find it lined with civilians who had flocked there to try and get off the ship. Anything that could fly had already left, and they now stood about like lambs awaiting the slaughter.

Rains brought them in quickly, and the civilians quickly parted as they came in to land. As they put down, they saw a pulse soar past their position. Taylor opened the side doors, and screams rang out from all around them. Taylor knew he didn't need to say a word to his own people; they knew what to do. He jumped out from the copter and into the crowds of desperate and terrified people.

He could already hear the screams of pain beyond those of just panic as the Mech pulse cannons fired. He could see the flashes of light above, but the civilians blocked their line of sight.

"Everyone down on the ground! Down on the ground now!"

He grabbed the nearest woman and pushed her down and began doing the same to those around her while continuing to yell, "Get down!"

The civilians gradually began to comply, but they still cried and wailed. As they did so, he caught sight of one of the first Mechs and took aim. It saw him in the same moment and began to pivot and train its pulse cannon on him, but he had already squeezed the trigger and let out a controlled burst into its head.

"Wait!" he heard a voice cry.

He looked around and saw a young man running towards their ship in a desperate attempt to reach safety. As he got halfway, a pulse struck him in the back and passed through his body with no resistance at all. It then brushed off the thick frontal armour below where Eddie was still sitting in the cockpit.

The man dropped to his knees. There was a hole through his body big enough to put a fist through. He was already dead when he collapsed to the deck. Taylor saw particles of another pulse brush past him where a shot had struck his shield and burst on impact. It was all the motivation he needed to turn back towards his enemy.

There were still civilians all around him and nowhere

for him to take cover. Neither could he easily get through them while as many pulses were hitting them as were coming towards his own people.

Only way is up, he thought.

Taylor took a quick step forward and fired his boosters so that he was launched forward over the crowd. He aimed himself at one of the Mechs like a rocket with his shield tilted forwards. The creature had no time to respond. He struck it head on and went crashing head over heels, as it too was knocked onto its back.

Taylor tumbled but managed to stop at a kneeling position and fired his rifle from the hip at the Mech who was trying to get back on its feet. His first two shots hit the knee joint of the armour, and the Mech dropped face first to the deck. He fired another three shots into its back. He quickly righted himself and turned to face the next enemy but stopped dead as a pulse cannon was placed against his chest. He had no time to react as the weapon fired.

The blinding blast projected Taylor through the air. He could feel several impacts on falling upon Mechs either dead or alive, but much of it was a blur as his body went limp from the impact. He felt dizzy as he rolled over a body and landed flat to the ground. He tried to get up, but he was disorientated and half blind.

Even though he was almost deaf, he could still hear a little of what was going on. Gunfire was almost constant from weapons on both sides. He got up to one knee but felt an impact against his chest. It smashed him back down onto the deck. He tried to get up, but as he raised a few centimetres off the ground, a Mech foot pressed down onto his breastplate and forced him back down.

His armour was all that stopped his chest from caving in. He reached for his rifle, but it was gone. The sling must have snapped when he was thrown. He tried to reach across for his Assegai, but he was unable to put his hand across his body for the heavy foot on his chest. The only option left to him was his sidearm. He pulled it from his holster and tried to take aim, but his vision was blurred. He desperately tried to focus, but suddenly the barrel of a pulse cannon struck his pistol and launched it out of his hand.

The impact nearly broke his fingers, and pain surged up his arm. He had nothing left now. He couldn't reach a weapon, and he was pinned in place. He looked up, watching the enemy weapon pan across and point directly at his face.

"Screw you, you alien scum!" he bellowed.

It was his last moment, and he knew it, but he wouldn't close his eyes. He wanted to see and witness his end. The light in the barrel of the cannon began to brighten as it gained power, and he knew he had just one second left and no way to avert death.

To his amazement, the Mech standing on him suddenly launched to one side and the weight came off him. The creature was barged out the way. The impact forced him to roll over onto his side, and he took a deep breath in surprise. As he rolled over, he could see Jafar stabbing his attacker multiple times.

Yet again saved by one I call a close friend, but an alien, nonetheless.

Taylor tried to catch a breath, but he still felt weak.

"That was foolish," said Jafar.

He couldn't help but agree. He had let desperation take hold of him and acted beyond what his training and knowledge would have otherwise allowed him, and paid a price for it. He looked down to see the front plate of his armour was smouldering. It was the thickest plate on their suits, and it had only barely stopped the penetration. He could see Parker and several others chasing down the last remaining Mechs in the room. Jafar reached down and offered him a hand. It was such a human gesture that it brought a smile to his face. Jafar was not unceremoniously hauling him to his feet, but offered assistance.

Taylor took him up on his offer and was helped upright. His head was pounding and his neck stiff. His arm still ached, despite the doctors having said it would be completed healed by now. He knew he hadn't given it the correct rest to heal. He heard a hive of activity and turned to see Rains' ship swamped with people trying to climb aboard. He could sympathise, but it wasn't helping.

He picked up his rifle from the deck and fired a single

shot that made them all freeze.

"Get down from the ship!" he boomed.

They stayed frozen, and he could see many were trying to decide whether to do as he said.

"Now!" he shouted.

Most of them slid back off the wings down to the landing bay deck, as he pushed his way to the ship and jumped up for a better view across them all. A couple of hundred people stood before him, and he knew their dead lay at their feet also.

"Take us out of here! Help us!" one of them yelled.

"Listen to me! Now! This craft is not going anywhere unless I say it does. It remains here because it needs to, and every second you hold me and my people up, the more of you will die out there."

"Take the children at least!" another screamed.

Taylor shook his head.

"The children?" he asked, "You think a child's life is worth more than any one of yours or my people? A child cannot fight for years to come. We're fighting for our survival today, tomorrow, for weeks, and months. Right now, the most valuable human being is the one who can carry a weapon and use it effectively. You have my word that I will do everything I can to protect you and the rest of the civilians on this ship. In return, I ask you stay here and not interfere with my people, my ship, my pilot, or me! Have you got that?"

A few groaned but nobody argued with him. He didn't like talking to them that way, but he knew the only thing that mattered now was time.

"Let's move!"

He jumped down from the ship and raced for the nearest exit. He quickly passed Parker who looked at the deep hole in his armour with disbelief.

"Lucky," she whispered.

"Damn right," he replied.

He carried on without breaking stride. Up ahead they could already hear almost constant gunfire from both enemy and friendly weapons. He had no idea what kind of numbers they were facing, and he had only a single platoon at his back, but he knew he had to head for the heart of the fighting and get stuck in.

"King, come in, what is your location?" he asked over the comms.

Nothing came back.

"They're jamming us again," replied Parker.

"Fuck sake. Every time we find a way to get around it, they screw us again."

Ahead they could see a line of bodies. Many were civilians, but amongst them were Chinese marines who must have come from the Lo Yang. Taylor shook his head as he noted their equipment. No body armour, old rifles. They were equipped no better than he had been the day of the first invasion. He remembered that time and how invincible the Mechs felt. There were just two fallen Mechs among the dozens of dead humans.

"They never stood a chance."

"And yet they came anyway, Eli? Stupidity or devotion to helping these people?" he asked. He could hear a heavy sound like a giant hammer striking an equally large anvil. They approached cautiously and turned a bend to find a Mech smashing itself against a large doorway, trying to breach it. Taylor instantly jumped into the corridor and fired a burst at the creature. His shots bounced off, and it turned towards him. It was one of the Juggernauts, but he knew it was too late to turn back.

He rushed at the giant Mech, and it appeared unarmed. But as he closed, it raised its arms. Lights flashed from pulse weapons running the length of his forearms.

"Shit!"

He held out his shield before him, absorbed the shots, and kept going. He charged full force into the creature, but it was like running into a brick wall. He stopped dead against it. He felt the Mech grasp the shield and knew he could not hold on. He let go and pulled out his Assegai. The Mech raised the shield to strike him with it like a club.

"Get down!" Parker screamed.

He ducked down, and half a dozen rifles opened up on full auto. The Mech was bombarded with fire. A couple of the shots appeared to penetrate and hurt the alien a little, but it did not stop it. Taylor could see the shield was about to come down on his head. He leapt forward between the legs of the Juggernaut, and the shield crashed down on the floor where he had been kneeling.

The alien spun around to continue its assault against him when a second wave of fire struck its back. Enough of the shots penetrated its thinner rear armour for it to spasm as the impacts were felt on its body. The creature tried to strike down to Taylor, but it was taking a continuous barrage of fire. Taylor could do nothing but hide in front of it or risk being hit by friendly fire. He watched as more than a hundred shots struck the beast, and finally it collapsed onto its back.

He was now able see his own people, and Parker shaking her head in disbelief at how much it had taken to bring the monster down.

"Hate those things," she stated.

"Everyone does," he replied.

Taylor banged on the door that the creature had been trying to breach.

"This is Colonel Taylor of the Inter-Allied Regiment."

"Who?" a scared female voice cried.

"We're from the Washington, and we're here to help you."

"We could just leave them be. Looks like they're as safe as they could be," said Parker.

The door unlocked and slid open. Inside were two women and a man. A pulse in the flank had clipped one of the women, and she sat squirming from the pain.

"Can you help us?" the uninjured woman asked.

"That's what we're doing," replied Taylor.

They tried to lift the wounded up towards the door.

"What are you doing?"

"You said you would help us?"

"And we are, by removing the threat. We cannot get you off this ship yet, and neither can we get you to the medical bay while the enemy still roams the ship. That wound looks pretty well cauterised to me. Safest thing you can do for now is seal this door back up and wait this out."

"But we…"

"But nothing," Taylor responded sternly, "All I need from you is information. You're the closest survivors to the enemy we have seen yet. What can you tell me about them?"

They looked dumbfounded.

"Come on, you know what they are. You must have seen them on the news. What are we dealing with? What kind of numbers have you seen? Do they have human agents among them?"

The eyes of the woman nearest to him suddenly lit up at his last comment.

"You saw humans working with them?"

She nodded in response.

"And their numbers? Any idea how many are aboard?"

The man finally spoke up.

"Last report I heard was more than a hundred had been sighted."

Taylor continued to present a calm image, but he was already getting a picture of how bad things were.

"You knew there were human-looking things out there, and yet you opened the door for us?" he asked.

They looked shocked and shaken.

"We just wanted to get help. This is my sister, and she's dying."

"She isn't dying. Lock this door, and don't open it again."

"Until when?"

"Just don't. I'll send one of my people for you when this is done."

Taylor turned to try and leave, but the woman asked, "How will we know it's one of you?"

"Rainfall," he replied, "You hear that word, and you know it's us. Now shut that door, and make sure it's locked."

She did as ordered, and Taylor carried on up the corridor.

"Rainfall?" Parker asked, "Why?"

"Because it's something no one else aboard would say, and it's something I'm sure we'd all like to feel. It just came into my head. Is that a problem?"

She shook her head. "What are you thinking?"

"That the Goeben wasn't taken over. It was theirs from

the start. The human crew could have been Krys agents. God knows there were enough of them in Germany. They came through with us to cause as much trouble as possible. They just made their move too soon."

"Too soon, Mitch? There are twenty thousand people on this ship."

"Yeah, and they haven't managed to take her out yet."

He stopped, realising what he was saying.

"What is it?"

"They must know by now they are done for, so they are going for maximum destruction."

"I thought that was obvious?"

"And how would they do that?" he asked.

She was speechless.

"Destroy the ship," Morris joined in.

"Yes, they cannot kill these civilians fast enough," Jafar agreed.

It was a cold and calculating assessment, but they knew he was right.

"All right, so they don't have any nukes or similar, or they'd have used them by now. How else can they blow this thing to hell?"

"Overload the engine capacitors," said Morris.

"They have measures in place to stop that from happening, surely?" Parker asked.

"Yes, but if the control systems are damaged or destroyed, they could overload without restriction."

"And then what would happen?"

"With enough of a surge, and the engines on these barges are big enough for it, they'd rip a hole right through the hull. Do enough damage, and they'd vent everything to space."

"How'd you know all this?"

"You were born in Earth's atmosphere, Sergeant, and I wasn't."

"Okay, I get it. How can we stop it?"

"At either end. Reach the engine bays and ensure they cannot access them, or stop them getting aboard the bridge and destroying the safety measures."

"Fuck," Taylor muttered, "we have no way of contacting the rest of the Regiment. We'll have to do this ourselves. I'll take Parker, Jafar, and three volunteers to the bridge. Morris, you take the rest for engine bay."

Morris thought the numbers odd, but he didn't question them. He pointed to three of the platoon and sent them forward to Taylor before carrying on and taking a fork ahead. Watkins, Abbot and May joined the three of them.

"You know the way to the bridge?" Parker asked.

"I do," replied Jafar, "Did none of you study the layout of the vessel?"

He appeared surprised.

"Yeah, I studied it," she replied, "but it all looks the damn same now we're here."

Jafar looked to Taylor.

"Hey, lead the way, big fella," he said as he shrugged.

He stepped over the body of the Juggernaut and picked up his shield. It was buckled in the centre so that as he pulled it onto his arm, the lower half curled away from him.

"Those things hit like a wrecking ball," he said.

"Yeah, well next time, don't get so close."

He turned to Eli with a smile, but she could see the concern in his face.

"I'll do what I can."

They passed through into a narrower corridor where the lights were flickering from gunshots that had struck them, and panels swung loose from the ceiling. Gunshots rang out in the distance, sustained fire from Reitech weapons. It brought a smile to Taylor's face. He knew it could only be their people dishing out hell.

Parker stopped at a crossroads and looked towards the direction of the fire. Taylor could see she wanted to head for it and help.

"No time. We don't get this done, and everyone could be done for."

They knew their own suits would protect them, but that was just a few hundred lives, compared to the thousands who would be lost. Jafar had only stopped after seeing them do so and waited for them to continue on after him.

"How much further?" Taylor asked.

Before Jafar could answer, two shots struck the wall

beside him, and he ducked back for cover.

"Those are ours," Parker said.

"Friendlies!" Taylor shouted, "Coming out!"

He took the bend to show a recognisable shape, of which Jafar certainly wasn't. A figure approached down the corridor; tall and confident and with a determined stride. As he passed into the light, Taylor recognised him as Major Moye. The tall black officer of the French paras was coated in blue blood and had a stream of his own dripping down the side of his face. He had just two others with him, one man and one woman. They were equally as filthy and blood soaked. They looked like they had been through a week's worth of fighting. All three had soulless expressions that were so empty Taylor could see they had witnessed the kind of thing he would not wish on anyone.

Moye had always despised Taylor, and yet all that hatred he was used to seeing in the man's eyes was gone.

"Where is your Company, Major?"

He shook his head. "Gone, all of them, gone."

Parker gasped, as she knew how many he commanded.

"What happened to you, Major?"

"We…we were first aboard. We fought hard, but there were so many of them."

He was distraught, and yet still held his rifle at the ready.

"So what is it you do now, fight or run?" Taylor asked quietly.

He struck a chord with the towering Frenchman who

at first took insult, and then appreciated what Taylor was doing. He seemed to snap out of his weary daze.

"What is your plan?"

"To save all those aboard from being vented into space. Are you with us?"

Moye didn't need to hear anymore.

"Lead the way."

We are nine, Taylor thought, *a distinct improvement.*

They carried on until they could hear cries of pain and suffering. They first reached a single wounded woman lying against a wall, with a young child in her arms. She was covered in blood. Her nose was broken, and a deep cut ran around her forehead. Several other dead lay around her.

"Help me," she pleaded.

None of them stopped.

"We'll be back for you," Eli said.

They all knew they could not stop and help, but as they passed her, the room opened out into a large communal room of some kind. Taylor was stopped dead and looked upon more than a hundred bodies scattered about the room where the Mechs had come through. Only a handful of survivors moved a little here and there. Taylor knew it shouldn't be any surprise to him, but he could not help but feel shocked.

Never had he seen such masses of massacred civilians, since he had rescued Jones from the alien camp. It shocked him for a few seconds, before he was reminded of their mission and knew they could not afford another interruption. He looked away from the dead and dying, and onwards to their path through. He stepped over bodies and put it out of his thoughts. He forced himself to think of the living. None of the nine questioned his determination to keep going.

"How far now, Jafar?" he asked.

"Not far."

Taylor shook his head, but as he opened his mouth to prompt his alien friend further on the matter, a pulse flashed into view and glanced off the rim of his shield. He ducked down into the cover of piled crates, and a number of other shots flew overhead.

"Is this it?" Taylor shouted over to Jafar.

"It is."

"How long do we have?"

"I do not know the operations of this vessel. If they have reached the central controls, then we do not have long."

"How long?" Taylor almost screamed.

"Minutes," Jafar replied calmly.

Eli looked to Taylor for answers. He knew they had no time for a firefight.

"We have to go forward. No matter what it costs, and no matter what it takes. Any moment now, this could be over, and it was all for nothing. We have to go forward, all or nothing."

As he said it, the two French soldiers with Moye nodded to each other and rushed out towards the enemy. They screamed some battle cry as they did, but it meant nothing to Taylor.

"Go!" he yelled.

The seven of them rushed out from cover and charged after the two who had led the way. The woman was hit by more than a dozen shots. The first two broke her damaged shield in two, and her armour took several more. Despite the injuries, she kept going and kept pushing to put one foot in front of the other. She took another eight pulses before finally falling, and her comrade fell soon after.

Taylor felt a bitter sadness inside for seeing their loss. He had never known their names, but felt the losses as if they were his own. It was enough to get them on the enemy's doorstep, and Taylor leapt towards the nearest Mech as a shot burst over his shield. He did not stop and struck the first creature dead on.

Taylor felt the power once again that he had grown used to as the creature stumbled back and landed flat. He fired several shots until it was dead before him and then continued on. He could see the bridge ahead and two Mechs working at one of the main consoles. He fired as he ran, striking both of them in the back. He knew he risked damaging the ship's systems, but the risk of not firing was far worse.

He drew out his Assegai and leapt forward against his next target; and carried on relentlessly when he saw one of the Mechs firing at Parker. She was pinned behind a console and taking fire from two directions. He raised his shield just a little, so that the bent lower half came in line with his head, and smashed it forward. The impact was enough to knock the Mech off balance, and it stumbled a few paces to the side before swinging its pulse cannon around for him.

Taylor jumped to the side of weapon and grasped it inside his shield, stabbing forward with his Assegai. It drove into the head and killed in a single blow. He let go, and the Mech dropped down dead. He turned just in time to see Jafar breaking another one's spine over his knee and then punching through the faceplate to finish it off. All was quiet now. He looked around for Moye and found him standing beside them with blue blood dripping from his own Assegai. He pointed ahead, and Taylor turned to look to the rear of the bridge where a man stood frozen and terrified.

"Captain Dokgo?" Taylor asked.

The man nodded, but he was shaking and rigid as if unable to move. Another person behind him stepped into view, and Taylor could see a gun in their hand pointed at the back of Dokgo's head. Taylor didn't even respond. He knew there was little he could do with his Assegai in hand at such a distance.

"Whoever you are, this will not end well for you," he said.

"She's with, she's one of them!" Dokgo spat.

"Yeah, I figured."

The woman was in her early twenties and strikingly beautiful, to the level he didn't want to believe she could be on the side of the enemy.

"Colonel Taylor," she finally said confidently, "You have already failed."

He smiled in response.

"Says the girl standing alone. You haven't blown this ship. You blew your cover early. You screwed up."

"You still don't get it, do you, Colonel? Every one of us you kill, we replace. A hundred lives for the price of one of yours, is worth paying."

"I don't see Karadag coming back from the dead, or Demiran," he replied.

She had no answer.

"So what's it gonna be? How do you want to die?"

"Take me to your leader, and I will not kill this man."

Taylor shook his head. "I knew you'd say that."

He released the grip on his Assegai and reached for his pistol. It was drawn and on target before the Assegai even hit the deck. It crashed down as he pulled the trigger, and a shot went right through the woman's forehead. Her blood splashed out over Dokgo. The Captain pushed her off him and looked back in gratitude to Taylor.

"Whoever you are, thank you."

"They came here to overload the engines, you know that?"

The old Korean looked fearful, and Taylor could see in his face that he knew, just as Morris knew what their intentions were.

"Then you got here just in time."

"Hell, yes. Did they get access to any of your systems?"

"I don't know. I didn't see what that woman...thing touched."

He turned around to look at the consoles, and Taylor simply waited for information; he had no idea what he was looking at.

"I...I think...no."

Taylor already knew what he was going to say.

"Is there anything more you can do from this end?"

Dokgo shook his head. "You have to get to the engine bays and shut them down in person."

"Do you have any means of contacting them from here?"

"Yes...normally, but we lost internal communications when all this began...we need..."

"I got it, I got it," Taylor murmured.

He jumped forward and led the others back the way they came until he stopped, realising he didn't properly know the way. He let Jafar pass him.

"Lead the way."

Jafar moved at an alarming pace that the others could barely keep up with him.

"Think we can make it in time?" Parker called out, breathlessly.

"If we don't, then it was all for nothing. So there is no if, we have to make it!" Taylor said firmly.

CHAPTER SEVEN

Captain Reynolds looked nervous as they rode on, with Corporal Berlin looming over them on the back of Kelly's truck.

"Relax," Kelly said, "she's the least of our worries."

"Maybe. How do we know these people are even friendlies? How do we know they won't just strip us all our weapons and supplies?"

"Gotta have a little faith left in humanity, Captain."

Reynolds said nothing, but Kelly was confident they were at least being led to a sight he was familiar with. They were on a straight road, and with no signs of a way off, when Kelly suddenly turned calmly in towards the thick foliage of a line of trees. Reynolds got anxious and sat back upright in his seat, expecting to feel an impact at any moment.

"What are you doing?" he pleaded.

But it was too late. They brushed the branches aside, and it seemed there was no resistance at all. Reynolds was speechless as they passed through a column of trees that looked like they had been grown as the boundaries of some kind of road. It was broad enough even for a tank to pass down. They carried on for a few moments when he finally got up the courage to ask.

"So this is the place?"

"One of them. There was always a chance Earth forces wouldn't be able to win in open battle. Just as we knew it when we fought on our home soil. Those with a little foresight planned ahead as much as they could."

"How many people know of these locations?"

"Not many."

Ahead there appeared to be another impenetrable wall of trees and foliage. Reynolds smiled, expecting them to go through it as they had the last one. However, twenty metres before they reached it, Kelly veered left through an opening. They began descending down an almost hidden route that took them under the surface and between a rock formation, in what had to be a man-made tunnel.

Another fifty metres, and they were in a clearing between rocks and thick forest once more. Two soldiers were standing guard ahead but stepped aside on seeing Berlin wave them back. Overhead a semi-transparent canopy stretched out across the trees that seemed to camouflage the position from the sky. Armoured vehicles were parked up and partially concealed around the opening, and they could see a bunker entrance of concrete built onto the side of a huge boulder.

Several of the vehicles had taken hits and were in various states of repair, with crews working in a relatively casual manner at the jobs. Half a dozen of the crew were at the entrance to the bunker; they were sitting about in chairs, smoking and relaxing. Kelly ran his truck all the way up to their position, but none of them moved a single centimetre. He got out and looked around. He found they were a force that appeared to be completely lacking in morale.

Nobody came to greet them or even acknowledge their arrival. Kelly got out of his truck and paced up to those sitting outside the bunker entrance.

"Who's in charge here?"

No one responded.

"I am Kelly, former Commander of the MDF forces."

"The what?" asked one of the women in a thick German accent.

Kelly could see Reynolds take offence at the statement, but he held up his hand to stop him from speaking any further.

"Years of fighting, our colony is old news," Kelly whispered to him.

He looked back to the group and tried to identify a rank, although most were wearing overcoats and tankers jackets with nothing on them at all. Others wore civilian garments. It was no surprise; the cold was certainly setting in.

"We didn't come here for your charity," stated Kelly, "We were fighting these aliens before any of you ever saw one or had a name for them. We know what it's like to be abandoned, and we know what it's like to lose your home. So don't give me that sullen, miserable silent treatment because I've seen it all before. Been there myself, and I didn't like it the first time. We came here to fight, and we will. So who the hell is in charge here?"

One of the men finally looked at them and spoke up.

"Right now, I am. The Colonel is wounded and undergoing treatment. Maybe he will make it. I do not know."

"And you are?"

"Lukas Becker."

Kelly squinted. He recognised the name and then looked a little closer at the man. He had never met him, but he remembered the description well.

"Captain Becker?"

The man nodded in surprise.

"Colonel Taylor sure told me a few things about you and how you fought together."

Becker suddenly jumped to his feet and extended his hand out in friendship.

"You knew Taylor? How?"

"Know him, still."

"Then he is with you?"

Becker looked around in excitement, as if he expected to see Mitch in one of the vehicles.

"No, but last I saw him he was leading the exodus off world. I have every faith in the fact he still lives. We know the fleet made it."

Becker shook his head.

"I hope he made it. I really do. But I'd still rather he was down here with us. No matter what we went through, when Taylor was with us, we always made it okay."

He took a seat back down beside his comrades.

"So you want to fight?"

"We do. It's all we have left to do in this world," replied Kelly.

"As acting commander of this...whatever we have here...outfit, I will accept any soldier who is willing to join the fight. But just remember, this is not a refugee camp. Everyone contributes to the fight, somehow or other."

"There are no civilians anymore, Captain. You're a fighter or you're a dead man."

Becker nodded in agreement.

"Then let me show you inside."

* * *

Taylor ran as if his life depended on it. He knew he could

probably survive through what the Mechs were attempting, but he was not willing to condemn thousands to die.

"Slow down!" Parker shouted, "You'll get us killed!"

He did not respond. He knew if he kept going they would all follow suit, whether they liked it or not. Moye got ahead of Parker and was gaining on Taylor who looked back in surprise.

"Don't let this be for nothing!" he yelled.

Clearly Taylor's words had gotten through to him.

Taylor said nothing but rushed on. Jafar had pointed the direction, and he'd simply gone until he heard otherwise. As he took a bend, he crashed into several others and was brought to a standstill. He raised his Assegai in shock but was delighted to see he had run into King.

"Colonel? You're alive?"

Taylor looked surprised by the fact, but he had no time to enquire.

"Follow me!" He carried on, and King rushed along at his side.

"Where are we going so quickly?" the Ranger asked, "These corridors are death to those who do not show caution!" he added, still carrying on at Taylor's pace.

"We have bigger problems, right now."

They ran like the wind. As they got close to the engine bays, they heard just a few shots, less than they would have expected. The corridor opened out to the engine bays where they found one of their own dead and five Mechs around him. They then passed a number of consoles and terminals and several more bodies of the enemy until finally Taylor stopped in his tracks. Morris was standing over the last Mech there and drove his Assegai down through its faceplate, deep into its body, to the cheers of his men around him.

Taylor had wanted to trust in the former MDF man but worried he would never be up to the standard.

Marines, paras, and rangers, and here a militiaman has done us all proud, he thought, and it brought a smile to his face.

"You did it, Captain!" Taylor said.

Morris turned, surprised to see them looking upon him.

"Is the room secure, are the engines safe?"

"They are, Sir."

Taylor sighed in relief. It was a strange feeling to not be the one coming to the rescue, and yet he welcomed it. It was nice to have someone else he could depend on. Morris seemed to revel in the bloodshed, but not in a bloodthirsty manner. He celebrated their triumph and success. He was a very different man to Jones, and yet, had already proven more than he first seemed.

"What are your orders, Sir?" King asked.

Taylor looked around at his own people. Fifty of them stood there. He prayed more had survived than that, but he was starting to understand King's fearsome expression and terror when they had met.

How many have we lost? He could not bear to ask and risk

breaking the morale they had.

"Morris, you and your platoon are to stay put and protect this area until I say otherwise. Moye you head back to the bridge and secure it. The rest of us, it's time to sweep and clear. There are still Mech sons of bitches aboard this ship. Not one of you shall rest until they lay bleeding out before you. The battle is over. Now we are the hunters. Split into ten-man squads, and NCOs take charge. Hunt those bastards down!"

The room quickly emptied, and as he paced out the way he came in, he realised he was left with only the five he had before.

"You ready for some payback?" he asked the three Privates.

"Yes, Sir!" one of them replied with conviction.

Taylor leapt forward and led the way. He had no idea where he was going, but it didn't matter. He was going wherever he could find an enemy alive, and that was all that mattered. He reached one of the main living quarters. Bodies were strewn about the place, and blood splattered across the walls and frameworks of the beds.

The accommodation reminded him of their new quarters aboard the Washington, but the lines and columns expanded as far as the eye could see. It seemed that thousands of people had lived in this one vast billet room alone, and about three-dozen bodies lay on the floor ahead.

"Poor bastards," said Parker.

"Yeah, but that ain't many. Not nearly as many as I might have expected."

"They must have run when the Mechs came."

"No, they'd have bottlenecked at the exits and been cut down. They must have been elsewhere or scattered throughout the ship."

"We can hope."

Taylor went forward and stepped between the bodies. He could see Mech footprints left in the blood, so at least knew he was going the right way.

"How many more of them do you think are on the ship?"

"Can't be more than a few dozen now, I shouldn't think, Parker."

"It's a big ship to cover with what, a couple of hundred marines at most."

"Yeah. We've done the hard work. It's time we got some help to mop up."

He reached an exit and took a turn back towards the landing bay they had first arrived at. Just at that moment, he saw a Juggernaut racing at him like a raging bull. Before he could react, he was tugged out of the way, and it stormed past unable to stop itself. Taylor looked behind. Jafar had been the one who saved him from being flattened.

"Thanks."

Jafar nodded and stepped out into the corridor in plain

view of the Juggernaut that had now turned back. It was stomping its feet as it closed the distance. Taylor leaned around the corner and emptied his magazine into the centre body mass, but it did nothing. The Mech continued towards them at a slow and relentless pace, in the arrogant knowledge that it was invulnerable.

"Go on," Jafar said, "Go and signal for reinforcements."

Parker went to move, but Taylor said, "No."

She looked at him, confused.

"We fight together, always. No one left behind."

He drew his Assegai and stood in the side corridor, waiting for Jafar to engage the beast. The Juggernaut began to gain pace, but nothing like the sprint it had been at before. They could hear the pounding impacts of metal as its feet landed, and it made its final charge at Jafar. But their alien friend did not take it head on. He stepped aside and smashed his hand into one of its legs so that it was thrown off balance. It fell face first into a tumble and crashed down the corridor.

He did not wait for it to recover but leapt after it and landed on top of the beast. He thrust down to stab it in the back, but as he did, the creature turned over quickly and struck out with one of its arms; smashing him against the bulkhead so hard the metal supports buckled. Taylor rushed to his friend's aid and smashed the creature's arm with the rim of his shield. It was trying to swing for Jafar once again.

The Juggernaut appeared to make no attempt to fire its arm-mounted weapons. They could only imagine it was out of ammunition after all the killing. Next the beast swung towards him with a straight punch. He held up his shield, and the impact landed above his shield arm and snapped the shield in two. It at least took the worst of the impact, but the fist still struck his helmet and snapped his head back. He staggered backwards.

Taylor felt blood trickle into his mouth and spat it out onto the floor beside him. He shook off his wrecked shield and looked at the Juggernaut with disgust. It was waiting for them to make the next move.

"This son of a bitch is going down," Taylor said firmly.

He knew he couldn't beat it with strength against strength. It was time for something different. Parker watched in horror when Taylor rushed at the creature, as if he were going to tackle it head-on. The Mech swung right for his head but at the last moment, he ducked to the side and under, thrusting his Assegai into the joint below its right arm. He carried right on past as it clumsily stumbled with blood gushing out from the wound.

Before it could gain its footing, Jafar leapt onto it and thrust his own Assegai down deep from above its shoulder joint so that the wound would meet with Taylor's. The creature jerked, feeling the pain. Jafar wrenched at the arm until it was ripped from the body, and blood squirted out across the wall. The Mech roared in both agony and anger that echoed throughout the corridor. It came back at Jafar with a clumsy but powerful strike.

Jafar backed off a few paces and finally thrust his Assegai at the wrist of the Juggernaut as it swung widely. The blade pierced right through before being drawn quickly back out. Before the beast could recover, Taylor ran forward and slid down on his knees and thrust up into the abdomen. His Assegai was embedded up to the hilt, but he lost his grip as he went past.

The Mech was still standing, and now Taylor was unarmed. He looked down and saw the creature's arm that Jafar had torn off lying bloody on the deck. He reached down and picked it up with both hands. The thickly armoured limb must have weighed as much as Mitch did himself. The Mech came charging at him, but he swung the arm like a club and aimed low. The impact struck the side of the Juggernaut's knee, and it buckled and fell against the wall.

Taylor did not let up. He swung the arm around his head to gain momentum and smashed it down with all his force. The Mech raised its left arm to protect itself, but it was beaten aside. He swung the arm around once again over his head. He held it at the forearm and used the shoulder pauldron as a weighted end as if it were a mace. The impact struck the heavily armoured faceplate, and it cracked on impact.

Despite the damage, the Juggernaut drove towards him

once again but was halted as Jafar's Assegai drove deep into its back. It spun around and reached for him, but Taylor took another swing at its other leg with all the strength he could muster. Its leg was knocked out from under it, and it went down like a tonne of bricks.

Taylor would show no mercy. He lifted the arm, smashing it down again and again as the beast tried to get up, but he could tell it was being drained of life. Finally, the sixth strike smashed it down, and he could see it was almost finished. He dropped the arm and looked around for Parker.

"Blade, Eli!" he screamed.

She tossed him her Assegai without hesitation. Mitch caught the blade, and in one motion spun around, and with both hands on the grip drove it down into the cracked faceplate, forcing it in deep. The creature was finally silenced. Mitch got back up to his feet, realising he had utterly exhausted himself in the fight. His knees were weak. His thighs were on fire and close to having gone rigid. He looked back and smiled at Parker, with blood between his teeth and dripping down his chin.

Parker didn't know whether to applaud or chastise him for his reckless behaviour. He turned to Jafar, who looked far more approving.

"Very good," he said in such a straight fashion, it made Taylor laugh.

"Good? Damn, what more were you expecting?"

"Next time we face one of these Juggernauts as you call them, we must kill it faster."

Taylor nodded in agreement.

"God knows how, but we have to find a way. We barely managed to take two of these things down. No wonder the Lo Yang's marines were slaughtered."

He threw Parker's Assegai back to her and reached down to draw his out from the corpse.

"If Demiran had used these, then the last war could have been a very different story."

"Wars are not won by one thing alone, Parker," Taylor answered her.

"Except you, perhaps."

He looked back and she was smiling.

"If it was all on me, then we'd have failed, but it wasn't."

Without another word, he went on down the corridor. As he did so, he holstered his Assegai and loaded a new magazine into his rifle. He prayed they would not face another Juggernaut, for he knew that one had almost killed him.

They carried on to the landing bay and found even more civilians squeezed in than before, and a few stragglers from the Ho Lang marines at the entrances guarding them. Despite the hundreds of people, there was little sound, beyond the cries of a few young children. The access door of the Mercury opened, and Rains stepped out to greet them, showing his astonishment at their condition.

"Looks like you've been through hell, Colonel."

Taylor said nothing but simply squeezed his way through to get to Eddie. He stepped up onto the wing and leaned in to speak privately with him.

"Have you got comms back yet?"

"Nope. Still jammed."

"How can you get a signal to the Washington?"

"I'd have to fly out beyond the reach of the jammer."

"Then do it."

"Well, okay, what am I telling them?"

"Tell them the ship is saved, and that we are conducting a final sweep of the last of the enemy."

"That all?"

Taylor nodded and climbed off the wing.

"Everyone back!" he shouted.

No one questioned him this time.

Eddie was off the deck in just thirty seconds. Taylor wandered over to where his own people stood awaiting him, leaned against the bulkhead, and collapsed down onto his ass. He had nothing left in him. Not an ounce of energy.

"You did it, Mitch."

"Was there ever any doubt we wouldn't, Eli?" he replied.

* * *

Kelly stood at the entrance to a barrack room, not unlike

the one Taylor and his people had been given on the Washington. He knew that space would be tight in the bunker complex, but he was glad to have a reinforced roof over his head and heavy armour at the door.

"You knew about this place all along?" Reynolds asked.

"Since it was established, yes. Although I'd hoped to never have to make use of it."

"Once again, we're underground and living in caves. I remember this all too well, and how it went last time."

Kelly nodded in agreement. It certainly brought up some painful memories.

"Last time we lived like this, we had the help of Earth forces. We had supply runs, weapons, ammo, and the hope of somewhere to flee to. What do we have now?"

"I told you when we began this, Captain. We aren't here to survive or win. We exist now only as a weapon. We live to make alien life hell. That is all we can do."

"Do you think that is enough to keep our people going?"

"Has to be. The alternative is death, and that option can be taken anytime you like. Just go for a walk, and death will soon find you."

"Commander Kelly?" a voice asked.

He turned to see it was Corporal Berlin.

"Formerly Commander, not any longer."

"Then what are you?" someone else asked.

Becker strolled in behind her and stopped in front of

Kelly, awaiting an answer.

"Retired."

"No longer. I'm the ranking officer here, as you know, and that goes a long way to showing how bad things are. But I am a tank commander. We have stragglers from a few infantry regiments here but nobody above a Lieutenant, and even she is little more than an admin officer who's spent her life filing and clipping her nails."

"Lieutenant Engel!" he called.

A short, thin woman appeared at his side. She had almost perfectly kept blond hair and not a mark on her skin. She wore fatigues that looked like they had never seen a speck of dirt, but she was shy, and that showed in her body language.

"We have to make do with what we have. What we have here is you two, a clerk and an old retiree."

Kelly could not disagree.

"But that is what we have, so fuck it, we can't complain. We have to get on with it. I need an infantry commander, and you are the most combat experienced infantry officer we have. As an officer of the...I don't even know what I am an officer of anymore, I lead whatever we have here, right now. Kelly I am giving you a commission to the rank of Captain, and you will report directly to me."

Kelly didn't look surprised. He could see Becker was more than a little burnt out by it all and needed someone else to shoulder some of the responsibility. He didn't want it, but he knew he had to take it. Becker turned to Engel.

"She is yours now, your problem. Make a soldier of her."

Becker turned and left in a casual manner, swigging from a hip flask as he strutted away. Engel studied Kelly's every move and expression. He could see in her eyes that she was more than a clerk, or at least had the potential to be more.

"Ever fired a rifle, Lieutenant?" Kelly asked.

"Not for a few years, Sir."

Kelly smiled. She could not have been more than twenty-five, meaning not since officer training.

"Don't worry, you will soon enough," he replied. He looked to Corporal Berlin. She stood almost a head taller than Engel and with the build of a strong man.

"Corporal, your armoury here, is it still stocked?"

She looked confused.

"I am not aware of an armoury, Sir."

Kelly smiled.

"Then follow me."

He led the way, and Reynolds and Engel paced after them.

"Sir, I was led to believe this was a fallout bunker for use by civilians and government officials in the event of emergency," said Berlin.

"Not really, Corporal. This was built as a base of guerrilla operations, should our bases and cities fall. Just as they have, and just as we are now doing."

"So we are not getting off this planet?" Engel asked.

Kelly looked back and was surprised. The young Lieutenant looked more than a little disappointed.

"Those who got off this world, you forget about them now, Lieutenant. I like to think they have made it somewhere safe. Somewhere they can rebuild and start over. But I'd bet money none of us ever see them again. This world has been left to us now, and we're on our own."

Kelly led them from one room to another, and it was clear to them all that he knew exactly where he was going. They passed a few personnel on their way, but it was largely empty.

"How many people do you have here?"

"At last count, three hundred and fifty four. That was before you arrived, Sir," Engel quickly replied.

"Then we must have about doubled your strength."

Finally, the room opened out into a large atrium five metres high. Corridors were either side of them, but up ahead a large mural depicting Taylor's defeat of Demiran. It was an overly heroic and motivational illustration that almost made Kelly laugh. He continued right up to the mural and touched it. His touch revealed a hidden access pad that extended with a palm reader.

"What is this?" Berlin asked.

"This is what's gonna keep us in the fight, Corporal. Where we just came from, that was merely the back door.

Welcome to Bunker Drachenburg."

He placed his palm on the reader, and a moment later, the mural split in two and retracted into the frame around it. Blast doors behind that opened soon after, and they were all left mesmerised at what they saw. A vast underground hangar stretched for half a kilometre and was lined with armoured vehicles and weapon stores. Thousands of Reitech suits lay in racks along the lengths.

"Wow," said Reynolds.

Kelly led the way forward. After all they had been through, he could see it was to them like walking through winter wonderland.

"How, how is this possible?"

"You see, Corporal, there is hope, just not in the form you would have expected it. We don't have ships. We don't have a way out of hell. But we do have a tonne of hardware and a capable army willing to use them."

"I need to get Captain Becker down here, Sir."

"Then do so."

The Corporal quickly got Becker on the comms, and Kelly overheard it all.

"Sir, Captain Kelly has found resources down here that you are going to want to see."

"Just catalogue them, Corporal. That'll be all."

"Sir, it would take me all week to catalogue what we have down here. It's beyond belief. Everything from ammunition to main battle tanks."

"What? I didn't hear that last part!"

Taylor smiled as he could hear Becker finally take Berlin seriously.

"You heard me, Sir. You need to see this for yourself."

It took Becker just five minutes to reach the entrance to the hangar, and he stopped on finding the entrance.

"How did we not know about this?" he asked.

"Guess it was need-to-know," replied Kelly.

Becker took a few paces forward and stepped into the hangar with two of his tank crew. They were astonished by what they saw.

"Before I was a Captain, I was a Commander," said Kelly, "I never wanted the job it turned out to be. When I signed up, being a Commander meant keeping order on a peaceful moon with a small colony. But times changed. We all changed."

"Sir, Captain Becker!" a voice cried.

They turned to see a man run frantically into the hangar and then stop in shock at what lay before him. It was such a surprise that he forgot why he'd even come there.

"What is it, Private?" Becker hollered.

"Uhhh....Sir...Sir...the Colonel. You need to come quickly."

Becker rushed out and followed the Private, and the others followed suit. They were led to the medical wing where they found Becker's commander lying on a bed with two medical staff stood over him. Becker went right to the Colonel's side. The Colonel was weak. Kelly didn't recognise him and did not even know his name.

"You're gonna make it, don't worry," he said, looking up at the two medics. They shook their heads.

"Don't give me that. The Colonel has to pull through this. Do something!"

"We're medics, not doctors. We have done everything we can for him."

"So what, that's it?" Becker shouted.

The Colonel reached up and took his hand, and that silenced him.

They all waited for the Colonel to speak, and finally he managed to at barely more than a whisper's volume.

"It's okay. I'm done. You know I am."

A tear dropped down Becker's face. It was the most emotion they had seen since arriving. He had appeared such a cool and calm officer. Perhaps too calm and carefree Kelly had thought.

"Who's this?" the Colonel asked.

"Kelly, formerly Commander of the MDF."

The Colonel smiled and then looked back to Becker.

"Then you are in good hands. Trust him."

The Colonel took his last few breaths and finally passed. Becker was at a loss for words. Kelly could not help but feel surprised that his last words were in support of himself. He had never met the man, but Kelly could see he meant more to Becker than being his superior officer.

Becker looked up to Kelly as more tears streamed down his face.

"How did you know him?" he asked.

Kelly shrugged. "I am sorry, but I have never seen this man before."

"And yet he trusted you."

Kelly shrugged once more. He was not able to explain it.

"He was my brother-in-law. The only family I had left," Becker added.

"Then I am sorry, truly, but he was not the last of your family."

Becker looked up, not understanding him.

"Your brother-in-law, you say?"

Becker nodded.

"So of no blood relation, and yet you called him family?"

"Yes."

"He was family because you chose to consider him as such, did you not?"

"I did. Always hated him for years and look, now I cry over his loss?"

"You made him your family. I am making you my family," added Kelly, "We have all lost the ones we love. We are all in the same boat. We might as well be family now, and we will fight and die as a family. I will call you a brother, Becker. Will you do me the same honour?"

He stretched his hand out in front of Becker and over the body between them. Becker had to think on it for just a few seconds before taking Kelly's hand and embracing him as a friend and brother.

CHAPTER EIGHT

Taylor sat around a table of key officials just as he had done the day before, and more times than he wanted to count now. He wanted to sleep, or do anything but be where he was now, but it wouldn't be allowed, not yet. He had to be debriefed and had to be there, according to Huber. He knew it was protocol.

But what the hell is protocol anymore?

"Colonel Taylor, are you with us?" asked a voice.

He looked up and around the room and couldn't even tell where question had come from, as he'd gotten so close to a moment's sleep.

"Yeah, I'm with you. What was the question again?"

"You described something called Juggernauts. Tell us more about them," asked Dupont.

"They're big, mean bastards. You don't want to go anywhere near them. Our boys are having a hard time against them, and they were definitely the reason for such high casualties earlier today."

He could see his straight talking and cursing was not something they were accustomed to at their table, but he wasn't ready to apologise or change his manner.

"Okay," said Huber, "Have we got a figure on our losses aboard the barge?"

Dupont was quick to answer.

"Current figures are four thousand three hundred and eight. Mostly civilians. At the moment, it is hard to tell the number of civilian and military losses. It will be several more hours until we have the exact stats."

Huber shook his head. "As well as however many on the Goeben were actually friendlies. We could have well over five thousand dead. Five thousand!"

The room was still silent.

"Five thousand in the wars on Earth would be unsettling. Uncomfortable, undesirable, but now, it's a tragedy. Ladies and Gentlemen, there are only so many of us left."

Nobody said a word as Huber took in a deep breath and wiped his brow. Taylor could see his unease at being the leader of humanity as far as they knew it. It was more weight on anyone's shoulders than he could ever imagine.

"Five thousand in a single day? We cannot survive at this rate. Things have to change."

"But how can that happen while we do not have a system of government?" Bletchley asked.

He was one of the few civilian representatives at the table, and they all turned to him with a look of scorn.

"The fleet, these people, they need…" added Bletchley.

"They need to survive!" Huber interrupted loudly.

"And there is more to that than…" Bletchley began to scream.

Huber smashed his hand on the table. It was hard and loud enough that it silenced Bletchley.

"Bletchley, you might have understood the politics of running a government back on Earth, but you have no idea what it is to manage a fleet under such desperate conditions as we face today."

Huber got up from his chair and paced around the room. He rubbed his chin and grumbled as he carried on pacing around them all. Taylor could see he was contemplating a painfully difficult decision, and everyone waited for him to make it. Finally, he got back to his place at the table and leaned over it.

"I have had enough of this bickering and arguing. I do not want to do what I have to, and never wished or hoped for it. We do not have a government, or any means of establishing an effective one at this stage. I am declaring this a military matter, and therefore the civilian authorities will adhere to military control for the safety of us all. As the ranking officer of this ship and the fleet, I am taking charge under martial rule until such time as the safety of this fleet allows a civilian government to be formed for the benefit of us all."

"But we have already begun setting up a regime," Bletchley stuttered.

Taylor could see in the man's eyes that all he wanted was his slice of power and that made him feel sick, but he said nothing. He could see Huber had the situation well in hand.

"Continue to establish your government, and maybe it will be of use. But it will submit to my authority until such time as it is fit to rule, and we are in a position of safety which permits a civilian government to operate."

"But...who knows when that could be?"

"Indeed, who knows? That is the very reason for making this decision, Mr Bletchley."

"Deputy Prime Minister..."

"Mr Bletchley!" Huber balled, "You might have been something special on Earth, but now you are nothing more than a single man who is yet to prove himself or be deserving of any more respect than I have given you. If you hadn't noticed, Earth is gone; at least for us. Whatever we do now is entirely new and built from the ground up. Our military leaders are decided for us because we are stuck in the jobs we have been doing throughout. As a representative of your government's parliament, I would expect you to have a key role in establishing a government, but that must be earned. Have I made myself clear?"

"Yes," he mumbled.

"Gentlemen, Ladies. We have had quite enough for now, but we have much to talk about. I propose a recess of two hours to reconvene at 1800 hours."

Taylor was the first to get up. He had been eager to get out of the room from the moment he first stepped foot in it. He went out into the corridor but felt a hand on his shoulder forcing him to turn back. He turned and found Bletchley standing behind him.

"Colonel Taylor, I must ask your help. You have had a good relation with the people of the United Kingdom for some time. Will you hear me?"

"No," Taylor said firmly.

He turned and walked away, but Bletchley ran after him and went past to block his path.

"Colonel, don't you see what is going on here? Both of our countries were built on democracy, and we have both fought to defend it in our own way."

Taylor shook his head.

"I didn't fight for democracy. I fought for our survival."

"But you would fight for it, wouldn't you? Just as your founding fathers did? Admiral Huber is seizing control of the people of this fleet without any authority to do so. He is tearing up all that we built over the last few hundred years. He's a tyrant, Colonel."

Taylor carried on walking, but this time Bletchley put a hand on his chest and tried to stop him in his tracks with physical force.

"Colonel…please…"

Taylor took a hold of his wrist and twisted until he released his hand from the pain and then pushed him up against the bulkhead beside them.

"Listen to me, and you listen good, you hear? I don't care for your politics. I don't care for what party you support, where you are on the political spectrum, or if you agree or disagree with a single military decision. You work at the will of the Admiral, and I will not have you trying to undermine his command or authority. The next time I hear anything of the sort; I will consider it mutinous behaviour and treat you accordingly. Do you hear me?"

He kept a firm grip on the man's wrist and squeezed a little tighter so that he squirmed.

"Yes, yes, okay!"

Taylor released his grip and carried on the way he had intended. Bletchley did not say another word as he left, but he knew he would be a problem in the future. Without even looking at his face, he could imagine the scorn and anger in the man's face.

He isn't one to forget, Taylor thought.

He headed right for his bunk. He knew if he didn't get sleep soon he would drop where he stood. When he reached their billets, he found Silva waiting for him at the entrance as he had before.

"Don't you ever sleep?" Taylor asked him.

"I get what I need."

It was clear Silva wanted or needed to talk to him, so he stopped and waited for him to continue.

"Sir, I have our casualty list."

Taylor nodded for him to continue.

"Sixty-four dead, twenty-one wounded."

Taylor shook his head. "That's about a quarter of our strength wiped out just like that, in a day?"

"Yes, Sir," replied Silva sombrely. Taylor tried to move on, but Silva placed a hand gently on his shoulder, causing him to stop.

"We can't carry on like this anymore," Silva added, "We take on the worst shit missions every time they come up, and pay a dear price for it, now more than ever. We keep this up, and there won't be anything left of the Regiment."

"So who would you have do the job we do?" he asked, "We have the greatest fighting force in the fleet and an amalgamation of some of the best soldiers and marines from around the World."

"Right now we do, but not if we carry on down this road."

"We're at war. We can't fight a war without losses, but neither can we continue onwards without replacing those losses."

Silva waited for him to continue, as if expecting some magical solution to their problem.

"It's time we did some recruiting and replenished the ranks."

"But how? Where do we get them from?"

"There are three million souls in this fleet. Some of them will be up to the task."

"People yes, but not elite fighting men and women."

"We can't be too fussy anymore. We can only do what we can with the resources we have. You leave it to me."

He carried on towards his bunk and simply jumped in, without even taking his boots off. He thought of those he had lost. He didn't even know who of his friends and comrades were dead yet. But he thought of how helpless he felt. There was nothing for him to do. No family to contact, no chance of a proper burial on home soil. He thought of recommending medals to both those who survived and posthumous ones, but it seemed so redundant.

"Colonel Taylor, Sir?"

He recognised Watkins who had fought beside him earlier that day. He lay flat on his bed and programmed an alarm on his watch as he replied.

"What is it, Private?"

"We're going to make it, aren't we, Sir?"

"In what way?"

"We're going to make it home, aren't we?"

It was a nice thought, and Taylor couldn't bear to disappoint him.

"Humanity was born to live on Earth, and someday we'll return," he finally replied.

It was a deliberately vague, if somewhat still hopeful answer, and he hoped it would be enough for Watkins, but no response came.

"You stick with me and keep doing what you're doing, and all will be fine."

With that, he shut his eyes and fell asleep in just a few seconds. Next thing he knew his alarm was buzzing. He'd had no dreams that he could remember, and it felt as if he'd only laid down two minutes ago. He sat up, but there wasn't quite enough headroom, so he had to slough. He groaned, as he had no choice but to get out and stand up. His body was aching and stiff, but he actually felt surprisingly well rested. Then he remembered he was due back in session with the leaders of the fleet.

Ah shit, not again!

He turned around and saw an officer approaching. He smiled for a moment, thinking it was Jones, but as he rubbed his eyes and began to focus properly, he could see it was Captain Morris and remembered Jones was no longer of this world.

"Well, that's a downer," he muttered.

Morris overheard him as he neared, "Nice to see you, too, Colonel."

"Forget about it. I was in another world."

"How was it? Think I can join you there?"

Taylor nodded in agreement. "If only."

"Has Silva given you the casualty list?"

Taylor nodded and grimaced at the thought of it.

"Most of them I never got an opportunity to know or even learn their names," replied Morris, "But you have my word, I will do my utmost to ensure respectful burials and a service fitting of their bravery."

"Thank you."

He carried on past Morris, heading for the door at a shambling pace of a man who did not want to go where he must.

"You're the right man, you know," Morris said.

Taylor turned around surprised. He did not understand.

"To be advising the leaders of the fleet. You're the right man for it."

"Why?" he asked out of curiosity.

"Because there are men and women with great leadership skills, but you bring more heart and soul to the table of any situation than they can hope to imagine."

"Stop kissing my ass, Captain," he said with a grin.

"I mean it. We got this far because of you, Colonel, and don't you forget it. Trust your gut. It has gotten us all as far in life as we have. Don't stop doing that now."

Taylor nodded in agreement and turned to leave. He still wasn't sure how much he believed Morris, but it brought a smile to his face and instantly made him feel better about the day. It wasn't long before once again he was stepping into the room of high-ranking officers and civilian officials. He was the last one to arrive. He knew he was late by a few minutes, but no one dared say a word. They looked at the dry bloodstains on his uniform that were both his own and the enemies, but again said nothing. Everyone waited for Huber to speak.

"Taylor, we were just discussing our agenda."

"For what exactly, Sir?"

"For the entire fleet. I am posing the question, what do we do now? We made it this far, and we seem to be safe for now. But what are our ambitions? What avenue do we want to pursue now?"

It was the big question none of them had an answer to, and Taylor was no exception, yet they all looked to him.

"I hate to say it, Colonel," Dupont added, "but it was you and your alien friend who got us out here, and we are all very grateful for that. You saved millions of lives. But you must have had some idea or intention for what we could do when we got this far?"

Taylor shrugged and shook his head.

"You see," Bletchley quickly joined in, "He's just a dumb soldier who jumped first and leaves us with the consequences!"

Nobody doubted Bletchley's assessment of the situation even though it made Huber shudder to hear him being quite so repulsive.

"Well?" Bletchley asked Taylor.

"Well what?"

"What have you got to say for yourself?"

"Well, I ain't no soldier, I'm a marine. And you ain't no Prime Minister, just an asshole."

Huber laughed, and several joined in which belittled Bletchley to the level he slumped back in his chair.

"In all seriousness, Taylor. For whatever reason we have arrived here, now we have some big questions that need answering. We have to start working together. So, Taylor, I don't care what ideas you did or did not have, start thinking. Where do we go from here?"

The room looked to him for answers, as if he was their great big hope for an answer to all their prayers. It was a responsibility he never wanted. He took a deep breath and thought about it for a moment. He laid out all of the options in his head as though he were planning tactics on a battlefield, and finally he spoke.

"Seems to me we have just three options..."

All eyes were stuck on him, awaiting a miracle answer.

"Option one. We can try and find a way home. That would make coming out here pointless at this stage, and we'd be annihilated. Option two. We continue to operate as a fleet and stay on the move so that we are hard to track, and carry on living like we are right now. Finding resources to keep us active and alive will be tough, and we risk running out of gas in the middle of space somewhere and not being able to do a thing about it..."

He paused for some time.

"And option three?" Huber asked anxiously.

"We find a replacement Earth. A planet that can sustain life and we can rebuild on. Somewhere with the resources to keep us going."

Nobody said a word for a full minute while they considered that last possibility.

"Are those really the only options we have?"

Taylor nodded to the Admiral.

"Not that I am glad we have not come to a quick conclusion here, but I can't say I am eager to pursue any of them."

"No, Sir. I wasn't eager to fight an almost unbeatable enemy. I wasn't keen to go into space at all. And I certainly never wanted to leave Earth behind. We have to work with the hand we've been dealt."

"The hand you dealt us," added Bletchley.

"Yes," Taylor replied, "The hand that kept you alive so that we could be here today to make this decision. I don't like it anymore than you do, but I'd do it again. We have to accept that we lost. We gave Erdogan everything we had to give, and he brushed us off like we were nothing. He isn't Karadag, and he isn't Demiran. He is an entirely different kind of bastard who is smarter, faster, stronger, and with a far greater force than we had ever seen. We lost. I lost. Does that make you feel any better?"

Taylor never thought he would hear the words come out of his mouth. Losing was a prospect as alien to him as his friend Jafar was.

"I went toe to toe with Erdogan, and he beat me as easily as he beat the armies of Earth. I would never wish to face him again, nor wish it on any man."

It was in this moment those around the table finally began to appreciate how dire their situation was. They had relied on Taylor for so long that his acceptance of defeat and assessment of their situation hit them hard.

"So three options?" Dupont asked, "One that sees us dead, one probably dead, and one with a new chance at life? Seems pretty simple to me."

Huber nodded.

"I wish it were that simple. Do you know how rare habitable planets are? We'd be lucky to find one in ten years of searching."

"Maybe," said Taylor, "or maybe our luck hasn't entirely run out. So we set our overall mission to find a planet we can live on. Up till then, we are living the only other option; option two. Maybe we get lucky, or maybe we at least get a few months or a few years of peace aboard these ships."

"How long can we last out here?" Bletchley asked.

"This exodus, as desperate as it was, had been well planned. We have refinery ships, factories, and processors. We can mine a few places along the way that won't be hard to find and go on for a few decades easily, providing the fleet remains intact, as we know it. The incident with the Goeben earlier cast major doubts on the security and longevity of this fleet. Those are doubts we must overcome."

Taylor didn't like having the responsibility placed on his shoulders one bit, but he knew he was only stating the obvious. It was the only course of action they could take.

"Okay, show of hands," said Huber, "Do we follow Colonel Taylor's plan, to search for a planet we can settle on? This is a mission that could take us many years, if it ever succeeds at all. But if we do it, and let every person in the fleet know it, at least they will have hope; that somewhere down the line we might rebuild our homes on some new version of Earth, as farfetched as that may be."

Every hand in the room went up within seconds. It was clear that nobody had a better idea.

"Okay, motion passed."

"Sir, if I may?" Taylor asked.

Huber agreed.

"What do we know about our surroundings? What scouting of the system has been done?"

Huber looked confused.

"You think I would send another ship out or break up the fleet, after what happened at that old gateway or whatever the hell the damn thing was? We cannot afford losses, and we do at least have safety in numbers. If I send out scouts, and they are ambushed, you know how quickly those alien vessels move. There is a good chance we could lose any number if they go it alone or in small numbers."

"And to be in unknown territory without information or advance warning of activity, it's suicide."

Huber nodded.

"A few weeks back I would have agreed with you, Colonel. But we don't live in that world any longer. This isn't some Marine expedition."

Taylor said nothing. He had no energy left in him to argue.

"No. We have a plan now, and we will implement it, but first things first. Let's secure the damn fleet. I want sweeps of every vessel. Thorough sweeps. I don't care how long it takes; I want it done and done properly. I will not tolerate another repeat of the Goeben. I want Krys agent scanners operational and looking for spies within the fleet. Let's get this locked down, or none of us is safe."

That was at least something Taylor could agree on.

"Taylor, I am placing you in command of this purge. Yes, a purge. Purge the fleet of all alien presence."

"Except for one."

"Yes, except for one," he replied.

"On that note," added Bletchley, "You have an alien walking freely among the fleet when we have already discussed the dangers of such things. It has access to you and key officials, as well as the Washington, the Capitol ship of this fleet," he turned to Huber. "Will you allow this to go on, Admiral?"

Huber opened his mouth to speak, but a croaky and

coarse voice growled at the door.

"No one lays a finger on Sergeant Jafar, and nobody questions his loyalty."

They turned to see that it was General White. He was supporting himself with a crutch. He had a dressing around his head and his other arm in a sling. He limped into the room, and it was clear that he was in agony. Only his raw determination kept him going forward.

"Glad to see you up on your feet, General," said Huber.

Taylor immediately got up and offered White his seat, which he gladly took.

"Didn't know you'd made it, Sir."

"There's fight in me yet, Taylor."

White got as comfortable as he could and then finally glared at Bletchley.

"You were saying?" he finally asked.

Bletchley grumbled and coughed to clear his throat. "I was merely posing the question that..."

He stopped on seeing the look White was giving him.

"Good," replied White, "I am glad that is resolved. Taylor?"

"Yes, Sir."

"You have your orders, and you are in command, remember! You can't do it all, or you'll end up looking like me."

"Impossible," he replied with a smile.

"Delegate, Colonel. It is your responsibility to ensure it

is done, not to do it yourself. Delegate and then get some rest. That's an order, you hear?"

"Aye, aye, Sir."

They looked back to Huber for direction.

"Right now, this is about consolidation," he stated, "Repair any damage to the ships, and give care to the wounded. Clear all enemy presence, and get everything on the top line. You all know what you have to do."

Taylor got up to leave and noticed Admiral Huang heading quickly for the door. He raced to keep up with him.

"Admiral Huang, Sir?"

Huang turned to acknowledge him but did not stop so that the two carried on walking side by side.

"What can I do for you, Colonel?"

"Sir, I wanted to ask you something?"

"Go on."

"Would you have fired on the Washington or her support vessels? Would you really have fired on the fleet because of a dispute over command?"

"I am not sure that it matters anymore, Colonel, for that time has been and gone. What concern is it of yours?"

"I just want to know who I can rely on when the shit hits the fan. Because if you're the kind of back stabber who would fire on his own people, then you're no better than the Krys agents who could turn on you at a moment's notice."

Huang suddenly stopped, and Taylor could see his was utterly shocked that anyone had dared speak to him in such a way.

"Are you questioning my loyalty?"

"Yes I am," Taylor replied sternly, "I've dealt with enough shit from enough people to know I need people at my back who I can rely on. I know I can rely on Admiral Huber and General White. Sometimes they can be sons of bitches, but that's okay. So are you the kind of officer who can be a son of a bitch or a real murdering bastard?"

Huang didn't know how to respond.

"Here's how it's gonna be. I'll respect your rank and command while you act in a manner deserving of it. The moment you turn on our people, and I do mean our people, by that I mean every person in this fleet, I will end you."

Taylor then carried onward and left Huang standing speechless in the corridor. As Taylor walked away, he heard Huber step up to the man and say, "You listen to Taylor. Many men haven't and paid the price."

Taylor didn't want to pick a fight. He only hoped his comments would be enough to keep Huang in line. The loss of his own people that day made him truly appreciate how valuable all their lives were, and how they could not afford to fight one another. He walked on down to the galley to get some much-needed food. As he entered, he could see Eli Parker sitting alone and deep in thought. So much so, she didn't even notice his presence.

He simply stood and watched her for a moment. Her shirt had a long line of stitches where she had recently repaired it. Her hair was tied back, and a cut on her forehead was covered over with a small dressing. Her knuckles were red from the chafing of her gloves, and yet he looked down to see her boots were polishing to a mirror finish. Every attention she had made to keep up her presentation, despite the raggedness it could not conceal. It brought a smile to his face that she tried so hard. But he wondered then if it was simply training kicking in or if she really cared.

Somebody paced up beside him and stopped shoulder to shoulder. He turned to see that it was Major Moye.

"You care about your people more than I was led to believe," he stated, "I judged you by your reputation."

"Really? And what is that?"

"Many things, and some that are true, but I was led to believe you threw away life for your own personal glory. I see now that is not the case."

He offered out his hand, and Taylor gladly accepted it.

"How are your people doing, Major?" he asked.

He shook his head. "Not good. I've got thirty-eight left of a Company. Maybe a few more will recover. Look at me, a Major in charge of a platoon."

"Been there, and it's not a happy place. We all paid a heavy price today, your people more than most. I won't lie. We aren't a lot better off ourselves. I would offer you a position within my Regiment, but the truth is, we need competent combat officers such as yourself. We need field officers."

"But with so little left to command?"

"It's time to replenish the ranks, Major. We've got three million people in this fleet. The vast majority are civilians. Many are needed for vital occupations, but a lot are not. It's time we started recruiting and getting some fresh blood into our ranks."

"And you think we can do it? You think we can train up a new generation? I have so many losses I need to replenish, that by the time I were through, I would not recognise my own Company. They would be greener than you can imagine."

"Not with us to guide them. We don't have a choice in the matter. Train up new fighters or simply run out. Come on, join me."

He went forward and took a seat before Parker. As she looked up and saw him, her face suddenly lit up as if all colour was restored to it. Within a second of sitting down, a plate of food was slid before him from Abbot who took a seat beside him and several others the other side. It was like a family sitting down for their meal just as it always had been, and that gave Taylor hope.

CHAPTER NINE

Becker looked like a stone statue as he stood opposite Kelly. They were listening to the other officers bicker and argue over the next course of action.

"Captain, what do you think?" one of them asked Becker.

He finally turned and looked at the man.

"I want them to suffer."

That was all he said.

"Now we're talking," replied Kelly, "You, what was your name again?" he asked the man who had finally drawn a word from Becker.

"Lieutenant Oster."

"And you?" he asked as he pointed at the next one.

"Lieutenant Thalberg."

He only looked at the last, expecting him to answer.

Lieutenant Decker."

"You're all tank commanders, is that right?" Kelly asked.

They nodded in acknowledgement.

"So, without meaning any offence. You have fought the wars from the confines of armoured vehicles in squadrons of what, hundreds of other vehicles in regular formations, and taking orders from a central command? What the hell do you know about fighting a guerrilla war?"

"How dare you..." Decker began.

"No!" Becker shouted and slammed his fist down on the table.

They were silenced.

"Kelly is right. It doesn't lessen what any of us have done these past years, but he does highlight a major flaw in our knowledge and abilities to take on this kind of fight."

"Well what do we do?" Oster asked.

"Rely on the only man here who actually knows what he's talking about," he said, looking towards Kelly.

"That old man? He isn't one of us. He isn't even a soldier anymore," Oster complained.

"Neither are you," said Becker, "We still have our uniforms and some hardware, but there is no army, and no government. We're a bunch of survivors who have come together for the apocalypse. Whatever ranks we hold, and whatever you think you might be entitled to, it doesn't mean anything anymore. None of it matters. All that matters is what skills you have and what ability and resolve to use those skills. Am I right?" he asked Kelly.

"But we're a few hundred against whole armies," said Oster.

"God is not on the side of the big battalions, but of those who shoot best," replied Kelly.

"Great, another piece of philosophy. That's not going to win any battles, is it?" asked Oster, "What help is God? He hasn't done anything for us this far."

"Maybe not," said Decker, "but Kelly is right in the sentiment at least."

"Thalberg, what do you think?" Becker asked, "You haven't said a word."

"If Kelly is skilled at this sort of fighting, then we must rely on his judgement."

It was the decider.

"Okay," said Becker, "I want to hit these alien bastards ASAP. I don't want them thinking the World went out without a fight. Kelly, I am putting you in charge of organising and planning the first attack. I want to be involved in the process from start to finish, and will have ultimate say in what does and does not happen. Are we clear?"

"You got it, Captain."

"Then let's get started."

"Okay. First thing's first. This base we have here, the Drachenburg. It is a good strong base of operations. It has a wealth of resources and can sustain us for some time. But none of that will matter if the enemy gain knowledge of its presence. Nothing will stop them from busting this bunker. We cannot take them in a straight up fight. You can't think of yourselves as regular soldiers anymore. You do not present yourselves for battle, and you never give your position away. Every action we make takes place at a minimum of five klicks from this facility. Do I make myself clear?"

They all nodded in agreement.

"That must be an absolute blanket rule. We do not take shots at passing craft. We do not attack passing convoys or troops within that area. Now this is a pretty isolated place, so I wouldn't expect us to see much of them out here, but even so. Nobody fires a weapon or engages the enemy within five klicks unless their lives are in danger. If this facility is discovered, then we are likely finished."

"It's going to be pretty hard to use our armour if we have to be so secretive."

"That's right, Oster, but our advantage lies in the element of surprise. Your tanks didn't win the last war in a stand up fight; remember that. We will have use of them yet, but they will not be the principal tools of our forces. We are all going to have to live and fight very differently. When I arrived here, you had a tank and personnel guarding the road several klicks out, is that right?"

"It is," Becker confirmed.

"We need them to carry on in their duties to watch and observe. However, those I met were set up for a trap that would guarantee combat, should any enemy forces take that road."

Becker nodded in agreement.

"That won't do at all. You must open road access and conceal those forces far better, so they may monitor any enemy presence but are not obliged to engage them."

"So we let the enemy walk right by, instead of blowing them to hell?"

"Listen and learn, Oster," said Becker.

Kelly took in a deep breath, realising he had an uphill battle to break them of their ways.

"Yes. You may destroy an enemy vehicle or two that you encounter, but many more will follow. Remember, we cannot afford to be swamped by enemy forces. We engage them at the time and place of our choosing. In every encounter we must control the ratio of forces, the ground, and the timing."

"And you think you can do that?"

"We have to, Oster. It's the only way we can fight this enemy and stand a chance."

"All right, then layout your plan."

"First thing I need is information. What enemy have you encountered? Their strength, position, and type of forces."

"At present, it's just small aircraft, and that's about it," said Decker.

"The big stuff is probably heading for the cities to

secure them," Becker added.

"Okay, we start small. Low risk. That's how this gets started. It doesn't matter if we kill just one alien or take down one vehicle. The important thing is we get it done right from the start and get away clean. Above all else, it is absolutely essential that everyone in this...whatever we have here...understand the most important thing is to maintain the secrecy of this location. That means nothing compromises it."

They all nodded as if they knew what that meant.

"That goes beyond the obvious, Gentlemen. That means NEVER compromising. If you have to not shoot because it will compromise our position, you don't. If you have to leave someone behind rather than compromise our location, you do. In fact, you put a bullet into them so that they don't compromise it. Do you understand?"

Their automatic agreement to everything he said stopped when they realised the cold hard truth of what he was saying.

"Don't think for a moment I am exaggerating," he added, "The individual now means nothing. Everyone is expendable to maintain the security of this facility. But it isn't because we are protecting civilians. There are no civilians any longer. The existence of this facility and this army we have is vital to ensure we keep being a pain in the ass to that alien scum. That is our goal from now on. We live to make their lives difficult, and to that end, this army must last as long as it possibly can. Do you understand that? Our individual existence is not important, except for being one of the soldiers. We never want unnecessary losses, but the individual is not more important than the mission."

* * *

Taylor stood before almost one hundred men and women who had been assembled as potential new recruits to the Regiment. They stood in what resembled a formation, as much as Parker could manage in a few moments of getting a hold of them. Taylor turned to look at Silva who had been in charge of assembling the first group of potentials.

"This the best you could find?"

"Not sure they are the best, Sir, but they are the first lot we found that were available to serve and of an age appropriate."

"And you think they are up to the task?"

"No," he replied bluntly.

Taylor smiled and was at least appreciative of Silva's honesty.

He turned back and looked at them. They looked tired, agitated, and uneasy. It was the look of a group of people after a long haul flight that had another connection to make. He knew the feeling well. They ranged from spotty teenagers to those pushing fifty. Half of them were well out of shape. Few of them lacked any fire in their eyes. They looked ready to lie down and give up. He looked back to Silva.

"You better hope you can find better than this, or we're in trouble."

Silva couldn't disagree.

Taylor stepped up onto an ammo box so that he could be heard. They were in the gymnasium of the Washington, one of the few high-ceiled rooms on the vessel, and where the sound echoed around the walls.

"I am Colonel Mitch Taylor. I am looking for volunteers to enter a training programme that if you pass, you could be a member of my Regiment. You will have an opportunity to serve the people of this fleet and protect its future. If you want no part of that, or think you aren't up to the task, turn around and leave now."

Many of them looked surprised but nobody moved.

"You heard me. This is your chance to leave. If you stay, then the only reason you get out of your responsibility is if you flunk out because you aren't good enough for this Regiment. So, I say again. If you don't want to be here, or you don't think you are up to the task. Leave now!"

One of the men in the front rank stepped out and walked away. He was shortly followed by several more until dozens were breaking rank. He was finally left with just half of the group that had been assembled. Parker leaned in close and whispered to him.

"Sure that was wise?"

"They were never gonna be up to the task. We just weeded out the first bunch of slackers, losers, and lowlifes," he replied quietly.

Parker stood back so that he could go on addressing the crowd.

"The Inter-Allied needs personnel, but it doesn't need just anyone. We require high standards. Those who stay and go through our training process stand a chance of becoming a member of our elite family. Those who fail or are not accepted will be sent back to the ships you came from and appointed other work. It won't be easy. Training will not be fun. The job is not safe or well paid. In fact, it isn't really paid anything anymore. We do this because we know we must, and we have a duty to all those aboard the ships of this fleet. If you think you can be one of us, stay, and give it your all. I wish you every luck and leave you in the capable hands of Sergeant Parker."

He then turned and left. Silva followed him.

"Think that was harsh enough?" Taylor asked him.

"Not a chance, but Parker will weed out the rest."

"Indeed she will, but I fear that will leave no one left at all."

"Then we will find more. There are plenty more people in the fleet. I won't lower the standard of our unit for any reason. We have to accept green marines and that's life, but it doesn't mean we have to accept shit marines."

Taylor went onwards and left Silva with them. He shook his head. He had spent years building the Inter-Allied Regiment. It had evolved over time as he had brought remnants of other units into the fold, but they had always been well-trained and experienced troops. Now he did not have that luxury. He knew he had to bring in new blood, or risk being whittled down to nothing at all.

* * *

Kelly took a deep breath of the fresh winter air. He flexed his arm in the Reitech suit and appreciated the power it gave after the weakness he had felt so many times facing the alien forces. The suit kept most of his body warm, but he could feel the icy breeze on his cheeks. A very light snow was falling now, and he could tell they were in for a hard winter.

The prospect was strange for a man of the Moon, and yet a few short years in the south of Germany had taught him a lot. Just as he always did, he had studied in every spare moment and knew his surroundings well, but he was still not accustomed to the cold. Seasons passed on the Moon without physical change in their climate controlled environments.

"How did they ever live like this?" Reynolds asked.

Kelly looked across to see the Captain was shivering. They had taken up positions on a crest. It was a good viewpoint of the valley that was a flight path to the city far to the south.

"Will this work?"

"As much as we can hope for," Kelly replied.

"How long do we wait?"

"There have been several low flyovers of this valley in the last day. We wait as long as we have to."

Kelly looked along the crest at the two-dozen fighters he had with him. Becker lay to his right, but he still wore his tankers gear as he had done before.

"This better work, Kelly," he said.

"It'll work, don't you worry."

They saw a flash up ahead, the signal for them to prepare for the enemy to pass into sight.

"This is it!" Kelly shouted.

They could hear the engines of the ship approach but could not yet see it. He looked across to Berlin. She was sitting in the seat of the anti-aircraft gun mount they had fitted into the back of Kelly's truck, and then almost buried in a hull down position and covered with foliage.

"Ready! Ready!" he yelled.

The ship roared into view. At the ground clinging altitude, Kelly knew they only had a few moments of opportunity.

"Now!"

The quad gun on the truck bed lit up the valley. It rocked so much the camouflage foliage shook off, and the light glinted on the surface of the settling snow. Tracer fire raced through the sky and led the target of the craft accurately. It was struck by two-dozen shots, and as an explosion ignited, it bellowed smoke. It then banked and plunged into the forest half a klick away. The troops cried and cheered, and Becker looked to Kelly with a smile.

"Not bad, not bad at all. You may prove useful yet, old man!"

Kelly got up from his position and pointed towards the crash site.

"Go!" he ordered.

They rushed towards the position at a rapid pace. The power and speed the Reitech suits provided still surprised Kelly, but he welcomed their abilities. He closed on the burning wreck quickly and found one of the wounded crew crawling towards him as he rushed over an embankment. Without hesitation, he fired three shots that went through the creature's chest. He carried on before it had even hit the ground.

A dozen of Kelly's troops reached his side, and they watched as two more of the survivors climbed out of the wreck. Every one of them opened fire and butchered the creatures with joy. Finally, the gunfire stopped as they stopped moving. Kelly approached the vessel, pulled a grenade from his armour, and tossed it inside. As it blew, Becker reached them and was out of breath.

"You did it. You really did it."

Becker looked surprised that they had taken down an enemy without armour, and that brought a smile to Kelly's face.

"Many ways to fight a war, Captain. Now we fight the only way we can. In the barren wilderness, the dark of night, and the isolated quarters of the land. This is our war now. We pick and choose the place, and we set the pace. Welcome to the Resistance."

* * *

A day had passed since Parker had been given her lot of potential recruits. Taylor strolled on down to see how they were doing, but when he arrived, he found just her and nine of them left. They were working on a pull up bar, and most of them were giving up as he entered. He could see Parker shaking her head in disappointment.

"Is this the kind of effort you'll put in when you're faced by an enemy that wants to tear your head off?" she screamed.

Parker noticed Taylor's presence and strolled over to greet him.

"This all that's left?"

"Yep, and they don't even come close to being good enough. If this was basic, they'd have flunked out by now."

"We just can't be as picky as we once were."

"But there has to be better than this," she said, pointing

to them.

Except for one woman, they had all given up and were panting heavily. Half of them had sat down, and several others were keeled over. Taylor stepped up before them.

"To be a marine is not to be a prisoner. You do attempt to impress us. You do your duty to the best of your ability because you know you must, not because someone is watching!"

He looked to the one woman still on the pull up bar. She was straining to do just one more and was close to exhaustion. She was slight, with died jet-black hair and tattoos running the lengths of her arms. Taylor pointed to her.

"You see the look on that recruit's face. She isn't willing to give up. She's getting angry, and she's getting mean. By the look in her eye, I'd say she hates us right about now, and is only continuing to prove us wrong!"

The black-haired woman tried for one more pull up again and was gaining height at a snail's pace but still trying.

"It's okay. You can stop now," Taylor said.

She finally let go and dropped down to her feet.

"What's your name?"

"Mia Moore, Sir."

"Sounds like the kind of name you'd front a band with, Moore."

"Yes, Sir."

"Moore, you're staying and continuing the training, the

rest of you; on your feet. You're finished here."

None of them moved. They clearly didn't think he was being serious.

"Get the fuck out of here!"

There were groans all around, as they began to get up and shamble away.

"Move!" Parker screeched.

They sped up a little, and they were just left with Moore now.

"You fancy yourself a bit of a badass, do you?" Taylor asked her.

"I do, Sir."

"And this bad girl attitude you got going. Is it real of just an act?"

"I've been fighting my whole life, Sir, just not had a cause to back me up."

"Well, you sure got one now."

He turned to Parker.

"What do you think?"

"She's got about as much discipline as a fighting dog, and just as much balls."

Taylor nodded in agreement.

"Okay, Mia Moore. You'll still have to go through a shit tonne of training to be as good as we need you to be. But what do you say, you wanna be in the Regiment?"

"I do, Sir."

"Then welcome aboard."

Taylor signalled for Parker to follow him across the room to where they could not be heard.

"That's a little premature, don't you think? We haven't tested anything but her willpower and attitude."

"That's enough. She's capable enough. She will handle the training just fine. We don't have time to go through six months of recruitment. We need a couple of hundred capable men and women preparing to join the ranks right now. That means you are gonna have to start getting ruthless with your selection. You know you can tell enough about a person in an hour. That is all you should need to give a yes or no. So what, if a few stragglers get through. They'll be weeded out at a later date."

* * *

"You think this'll work?"

"Trust me, Berlin," replied Kelly. They were storming along a country road in his truck.

"I sure would have been happier if we'd kept the AA gun on the back."

"Yeah, well that would defy the object, wouldn't it?"

She shook her head.

"Not long now," he added.

The line of trees was coming to an end up ahead, and they could see the bright opening that would put them out on an open plain for all to see.

"Don't worry. It'll work."

"I'm sure the first part will, and we'll surely get some attention. I'm just not so sure about the second part, surviving the experience."

"Too late now."

They burst out into the morning sunshine. Under the shelter of the forest canopy, they had not seen such bright light since leaving their homes, and it was almost blinding. Kelly kept up the speed, both as to try and get noticed, and not get hit. He felt the back end of his truck begin to slide and merely put more power down and pulled it back into line.

"That's if you don't kill us first," Berlin added.

They got a hundred metres across the open plain when a pulse impacted on the ground just in front of them. The truck dropped into the crater, ramped up the other side, and continued on.

"Damn that was fast!" Kelly yelled.

They looked ahead to see it was another hundred metres to the tree line.

"This is gonna be close!" Berlin shouted.

She knew there was nothing to do now but hold on and hope. Another two pulses landed around them, and Kelly swerved the vehicle to avoid the enemy being able to lead them.

"You see, moving target, they can't hit us!"

As he said it, another pulse skimmed the roof of the

truck and burnt off a corner of the cab.

"That was too close!" Berlin hissed under her breath.

A second later, they raced into the narrow clearing of the forest, and Kelly slowed the pace to a half.

"Have we got them?"

Berlin looked back for confirmation.

"Can't see anything...wait... there they are! Put your foot on it!"

He accelerated away as another two pulses raced their way. One of them struck a tree up ahead, and it began to fall across the road.

"No, no, no!" Berlin screamed.

"We can make it!" Kelly cried.

He put his foot to the floor as they raced towards the falling tree that they knew would easily crush the truck. They reached it just in time, and Berlin looked back to see it crash to the ground only a metre behind the vehicle.

"Way too close," she said.

"We're still alive, aren't we?"

"For now, Sir."

She looked up out of the windscreen and could just make out the shape of the craft flying overhead and following the route to the next opening. It was twice the size of the fighter they had shot down the day before.

"They're heading to cut us off exactly as you wanted."

"Good. Time for the welcome party."

Kelly carried on with a smile on his face, although

Berlin didn't see the funny side of their situation. A few minutes later, they could see the light ahead where the forest opened up once again, and the path came to an end in a rocky canyon. They almost reached the opening when they saw the alien craft descend into the opening and land in front of them. Kelly brought his truck to a standstill, and they watched six Mechs stride out of the ship to confront them.

They raised their pulse cannons to take aim at the truck, but as they did, a rocket trail zoomed towards the ship behind them. It exploded, sending shrapnel almost as far as Kelly's vehicle. Before the Mechs could respond, each of them was struck by dozens of shots from Reitech rifles and riddled until they dropped where they stood. Kelly and Berlin simply sat back and watched the show as the aliens were executed before them. Finally, as the dust settled, Kelly got out and strolled forward to the see the results of their work.

As they approached, a number of troops stepped out from their concealed positions, including Becker. He paced up to the bodies and wreckage, looking through it for any sign of life. The Mechs on the ground were dead, without a doubt, so he carried on up to the wreckage of their ship. Part of the hull was still intact but was twisted and burnt. A huge hole had been ripped in the side from the impact. He looked inside and saw a single Mech. It looked dead, but he fired three shots into its head to be certain. Finally, he turned back to Kelly and Berlin who stood over the bodies of the Mechs.

"Not bad at all, Kelly. Seven dead and a ship knocked out. No casualties or losses of equipment on our side."

He looked past them to the state of the truck and the roof that had been opened like a can of beans by the impact.

"Looks like you came a little too close there."

"Far too close," Berlin said, "We survived that more out of luck than skill."

"Yeah, well, I guess that's part of our lives now," replied Becker, "Luck. We do everything we can, as we always have, but we're gonna need a tonne of luck to keep this up."

Smoke arose from the craft high into the sky.

"This is going to attract attention."

"Good," said Kelly, "take up your positions. Let's get a little bonus out of this."

Kelly went back to his truck and pulled it off the road into nearby foliage, and then took up position in a well-concealed dugout beside Becker.

"Sure this is a good idea? We've taken out one of theirs. Doesn't seem like a good idea to hang about."

"As far as they know, one of their ships has gone down, and even if they radioed in what they saw, it will just be my truck, a civilian vehicle. They'll send another to investigate before deploying anything too heavy."

"You sure about that?"

"Yes, I'm sure, Berlin. You don't commit an army to investigate a single loss. This is our chance to expand on our work here today. Then we leave. A second ambush can work in our favour, but they won't fall for a third. Now listen up and be ready."

They sat and waited in their dugout for twenty minutes without seeing a sign of movement. Finally, Becker asked, "Why didn't you leave?"

Kelly looked surprised.

"What do you mean?"

"You're a civilian, or you were. You and your people could have gotten off the planet. Particularly if you pulled a few strings with Taylor. Why did you stay?"

"Why did you?"

"We're soldiers. We were there to defend our country."

"Yeah, so were we."

"And this country means that much to you?"

"Damn right it does. You truly learn to appreciate your own home ground once it's gone. I couldn't leave it again."

"But you know we're all gonna die down here. Maybe not today or tomorrow, but soon enough."

"Yeah, probably," he replied casually.

"So why?"

Kelly shook his head.

"I don't know how many more ways I can explain it. We're here. You're here. There's only one thing left for us to do, and we're doing it."

"You sound like Taylor," he replied.

Kelly laughed.

"Well, that can't be a bad thing. That crazy son of a bitch can survive anything."

They could faintly hear an engine in the sky.

"Everyone down. Get ready!"

It was almost half a minute until the ship came into view. It was the exact same model as the one they had destroyed and lay a crumbled wreck before them. The ship hovered above and circled the position, clearly investigating from the air.

"Come on, you alien bastard, land already," whispered Becker.

It slowly came in to a smooth landing, and as before, six Mechs stepped out to investigate. Kelly smiled.

"Predictable. They're like machines."

He raised his rifle to the shoulder and took careful aim at the nearest, squeezing the trigger so that a three-shot burst struck the creature and killed it instantly. Before it had even hit the dirt, another two-dozen rifles opened fire. The creatures were gunned down before they could loose off a shot. The ship's engines began to gain power to lift off and make a run for it.

"Bring it down!" Becker hollered.

The ship got a metre off the ground when a rocket streamed towards it. It hit one of the engines dead on and blew it off the side of the craft. The loss of one of the two engines caused the ship to go into a spin and crash back down into the wreckage of the first. Kelly jumped out of his trench and rushed to the wreckage. He pulled a grenade from his armour and threw it in through the breach in the hull, rushing back as it blew. Becker and the others ducked for cover when the explosion rang out, but as it settled, they got up and found Kelly was standing in front of the wrecked ship as calm as could be.

"Woohoo!" Becker shouted, "Nailed them!"

CHAPTER TEN

Taylor stepped into Huber's private quarters and saluted.

"Come in and sit down, Colonel."

"Yes, Sir."

"I have reviewed your report. Your conclusion is that the fleet is now free of all enemy presence?"

"I have been as thorough as is humanly possible, Sir."

"A number of the ships' Captains are asking for a guarantee that we are free of them. Can you give it?"

"No, Sir, but I can ensure you that we have done, and continue to do, everything in our power to ensure the safety of the fleet."

Huber took a deep breath.

"That's what I told them. I told them there are no guarantees in war, but still they ask."

"Then give them the guarantee, Sir."

"But you said you cannot give it."

"No, I can't, but that doesn't mean you can't say it. Sometimes people just want to be told what they want to hear. And sometimes it is best to do so."

Huber shook his head as he poured himself a whisky and then another for Taylor.

"You've had to play the politician for too long."

"Not of my choosing, Sir. But if it takes one slight exaggeration to calm the Captains of the fleet, so be it. What we need more than anything else right now is calm and clear thinking."

Huber nodded.

"You said you wanted to scout this system?" Huber asked as a rather open ended question that he was looking for an expanded answer.

"Yes, Sir. It's all very well that the fleet continues onwards, but we have many vessels in the fleet far faster than our average. Ships that could travel far and wide as we carry on our course."

"And you think it is safe to do so, to send out smaller scouting parties? Parties who will likely be too weak to take on any serious threat alone. Still too slow to outrun it, and all at the same time weakening our defence of the fleet?"

"Everything we do is a risk, Sir, and not making use of all our resources could mean us never finding new worlds and new mineable areas. To do this would spread our forces, but there is no safe option."

"Okay."

Taylor looked surprised. "Okay? You'll do it, Sir?"

Huber nodded.

"What the hell? Seems as good an idea as any. It's certainly true we need to know what we're dealing with wherever we are. I'll organise six frigates to send out in all directions, along with support fighters and such."

"Might I recommend a solid Marine detachment aboard each of the vessels, Sir?"

"Yes, but you will not be with them. Your place is here, Taylor. You are a good fighter, but out in the field that is all you can be. One man."

"Excuse me, Sir, but I believe my value in combat amounts to more than the sum of a single marine."

"Yes, yes. I don't mean to insult you, Colonel. However, your leadership skills and command are far more valuable to me than your individual fighting skills. Better still, I like to know I have my best man at my side on my ship when the shit hits the fan. So there it is. I'll organise the ships. You see to it that their Marine detachments are well equipped and of good number. But you may not allocate your own people, or any of the marines aboard this ship to this endeavour, do you hear?"

"Aye, aye, Sir."

"Then drink up, Colonel, you have work to do. I have already assembled the frigate Captains via commlink in operations room B. They await your arrival."

It was then Taylor realised he wasn't being asked his opinion on anything. He had been brought there to be given his orders. It had just been disguised as a pleasant chat and a drink with an inquest into his thoughts.

"Yes, Sir," he replied.

He got up, left, and went straight to the operations room as ordered where he found the projections of the Captains displayed at modules placed on the table in front of six of the seats. He did not recognise a single one of them, but he could see Huber had selected them from various different navies.

Wise move, he thought, after seeing how close they came to fighting each other so recently.

"I assume Admiral Huber has already briefed you on your missions?"

They all nodded in agreement.

"And you have designated areas plotted already?"

They agreed again.

"Then I am here merely to arrange Marine detachments for all of your vessels."

"We already have marines aboard," one of them said.

Taylor didn't even bother asking his name. He just went right into his response.

"The Lo Yang had marines, brave men and women who went into combat without hesitation. Barely a single one of them survived the fighting aboard the barge yesterday. Those who survived made it because experienced and well-equipped marines saved their asses. Now I don't know a single one of you, but that doesn't mean I have no care for you and your crews. Right now, if you get boarded by any number of enemy hostiles, you can be pretty damn sure you won't survive the experience. I am here to make sure we don't lose any more ships, and we don't lose any more people. Admiral Huber has given me full command and authority to equip and assign the Marine detachments to your vessels, and you will abide by my ruling. Have you got that?"

They agreed, but he could see none of them liked it, so he went on.

"I am not trying to pick a fight with any of you. I am not here to assert my authority and try and take charge of the situation. I want to see you live through this mission, is it that too much to ask for?"

Still nobody said a word, but they were starting to come over to his point of view.

"Good. I will have your Marine detachments and additional equipment for your own personnel despatched to you by 0700 hours tomorrow so that you may depart at 0900, as per Admiral Huber's orders. Thank you, that will be all."

He got up and left without waiting for a response. He didn't like having to organise the mission without going out there himself. His first thought would have been to allocate his own officers and personnel to some of the ships, but he could not do that either. He knew he had to find others he could trust.

Taylor put a call through on the Mappad device on his arm. A moment later, Major Moye answered.

"What can I do for you, Colonel?"

"I need your help."

"Just say when and where."

* * *

Kelly's truck rolled into the hangar bay at Drachenburg, with Becker on the back of the truck bed, to an excited crowd who cheered as they came to a standstill. Two hundred of the people were there to greet them and clapped and whistled as they got out. Kelly couldn't believe what he was seeing. It was more joy and celebration than he had seen since the last war had ended.

"What are they so excited about?" Becker asked as Kelly climbed up onto the truck bed beside him.

"We just gave them something new in their lives beyond fear of death."

"What?"

"The chance of victory."

"Victory? We can never win."

"The war maybe, but we can win many battles. And everyone of them is reason to celebrate!"

He raised his hand to call for silence, and after nearly

another minute of cheering, they slowly died down and listened.

"Today we destroyed two Krys ships and fourteen of their Mechs, to the loss of nothing more on our side than the roof of my truck!" he jested.

It brought some laughter, a rare and pleasant sight over the last few days.

"The enemy isn't invulnerable. They can be killed, they can be beaten, and they can feel fear. And that is what I intend to do. I want their soldiers to fear ever leaving their bases, for the chance they might run into us!"

More cheers rang out.

"Today's work is over. Well done to you all. We do this bit by bit. No grinding war that is always on our doorsteps. We fight them when and where we want, and then we celebrate our victories together!"

He jumped down from the truck and fought his way through the crowds to another truck covered over with a sheet. The crowd watched his every move and did not know what to expect.

"You all did well today. Now let's celebrate this victory, and every one that is to follow!"

He tugged at the sheet. It slid off and revealed a box truck with the rear door open. It was stuffed to the roof with alcohol.

"No way," said Becker.

"Dig in!" Kelly ordered.

The crowd went wild as he forced through, took a crate of beer, and fought his way back to Becker.

"You brought that with you?"

"A few of my boys did. I told them to gather all available vehicles. They gathered the delivery truck for the local bars. Just so happened it was out for delivery."

Becker laughed and Kelly passed him a bottle.

"This is hardly soldierly discipline," a voice said.

Kelly turned to see Corporal Berlin was standing behind him.

"No, it isn't. Times change. Look at these people," he said, "They need something to cling on to. They need some good in their lives. If getting slaughtered after doing some slaughtering keeps them going, then so be it."

He passed her a beer, and it was hard for her to refuse; she was starting to see his point.

"What are we now, Sir?"

"What do you mean, Becker?"

"Well, look at us. Tankers. We're a mix of forces of the Bundeswehr, retired Moon Defence Force, and there are a few others I don't even know who the hell they are. We have no command structure left, no Generals or leaders. What are we?"

"It is true we need an identity," Berlin joined in.

"Then we will make one. This place is what has brought us together," said Kelly. "The Drachenburg. Dragon Mountain, is it?"

"Something like that," replied Becker.

"Each one of these bunkers was named after a Schloss."

"So there are more like it?" Berlin asked.

"There are, but for the sake of security, I only ever knew of one. But you can be sure that wherever those other bunkers are, there are people like us keeping this fight going."

It was a heart-warming thought.

"So who are we now? Are we not the dragons in this mountain?"

Becker laughed.

"It's a little corny, don't you think?"

"More than a little," Berlin laughed.

"Yes it is, and maybe it's just what we need."

He climbed back onto the truck.

"Quiet! Everyone listen to me!"

They quickly calmed down but continued dragging out bottles from the truck.

"We are a community now! We are an army. Whatever we used to be. Wherever you used to call home, and whatever nationality you were, it doesn't matter anymore! Now we are brothers in arms. This is the Drachenburg, and we are the dragons of the mountain. Henceforth it is what we will call ourselves! We prowl these mountains. We stalk our prey. We are fire-breathing monsters. You all feared the aliens when they first arrived, as did I. They were terrifying creatures of immense power. Today we killed fourteen, without as much as a single shot fired in return. We are the monsters now. We are the creatures they will fear. We are the Dragons!"

The crowd cheered, and Becker shook his head at how absurd it sounded.

"You're pandering to the mob," he muttered.

"Yes I am," he replied without hesitation, "and isn't it exactly what they needed?"

It was hard for Becker to disagree, but he still smirked at the prospect. "Dragons? It's funny. Taylor would laugh if he were here, too."

"Perhaps, and yet he calls his comrades the Immortals. Is it any less pretentious?"

"No, but that was a name bestowed on them by others, and so they can rightfully continue to use it."

"Yeah, well, there isn't anyone left to praise our people's achievements, so we must do so ourselves."

"That's true," replied Becker cynically, "You're our leader now, Kelly. Any doubts I had have long been cast aside. I will call you Commander, and I will follow you to the very end."

"Just know that I didn't want this, Captain. I do this because I have to, and somehow it's worked out this far."

"You're a born leader, Sir, and I'd be a fool to pass up on that skill."

They turned back to look at the party that had started. Many of the others from the bunker had heard of the truck of beer and rushed to join in. Some were dancing like fools, and others embroiled in conversation as if it were any other day.

"Today was a great day. We couldn't ask for more. We achieved success without any cost," said Kelly, "Most days won't be this good, but let them enjoy it. And let's be certain to keep the stocks of beer high. We are going to ask a lot of our people over the coming days and weeks. They need to know they have something to look forward to. Something worth coming back for."

"And beer is worth coming back for?"

"It's not the beer that does it. It's this, this spirit, this excitement, and enthusiasm. Knowing the beer is here just reminds them where the party is."

* * *

Taylor stood on the deck of the Washington's loading bays. Before him was Major Moye and his people, as well as a number of other troops he had inducted into his ranks. It was just a small portion of the marines being assembled throughout the fleet. Taylor climbed up onto a storage box to address them.

"You all know what your mission is. I would be out there with you myself, were it not for the Admiral's express orders. With any luck, it'll be a walk in the park, a few days or weeks of moping about a ship with no excitement at all. Take the opportunity you have when not on duty to get what rest you can. You need it and you've earned it. But always remember, your job is to ensure the safety of the ship you are aboard. And to that end, stay sharp, and good luck!"

Taylor stepped down and went straight to Moye and shook his hand.

"Thanks for thinking of me, Colonel."

"Not like I had a lot of options, Major. Besides, in my own Regiment, you're the only officer I could trust."

"There'll be more. Give it time. Do you believe there is any chance of us finding a habitable planet?"

Taylor shook his head.

"I'd say absolutely zero. I figure this will be the first of a countless number of similar missions over the years to come. But who knows? Stranger things have happened."

"They certainly have."

"Good luck, Major."

Moye saluted, turned back to his people, and ordered them aboard the transports. Taylor wanted nothing more than to go with them. Despite not expecting them to find what they were looking for, it was highly likely they'd find trouble.

"They'll be okay," a voice said behind him. He recognized it as Parker and turned quickly to look upon her with his own eyes.

"You know I don't like sending others to do the dirty

work," he replied.

"What now?"

"Right now I only have two priorities. Scouting the system is something that is out of my hands, so I turn to the other. Filling the ranks of the Regiment. How is recruitment going?"

"Better, but far from great."

"How many recruits do you now have in training?"

"I accepted thirty-five, but seven dropped out in the first day. I'm wondering if we should even give them the choice of quitting."

"Yes, we must. If they aren't committed, then they aren't worth having. I will not have reluctant personnel in my Regiment. If you sign up with me, you're in till death or absolute victory."

"And if they don't believe the latter is an option?"

"Then we'd better ensure we have a good death."

"Is there such a thing?"

Taylor nodded. "Damn right there is, now, about this training. You're still in charge of recruitment, but seeing as I have nothing else of importance to do, I will be overseeing the process and getting involved at every stage. I want to know we are getting good people and that they have the best training. Show me how you're progressing with them.

"Mitch, their time is their own."

"No, they belong to us now. Until such time as they

quit or flunk out, their time is ours to do with as we please. Let's go."

Parker led him towards the bunkroom where they were now living.

"All the recruits I've taken on so far are from the Detroit."

"The Detroit?"

"It's one of the transport barges. They've started calling them after the cities they came from. There was never more than a single barge in any city, so it sort of makes sense. I figured we'd try and take Americans first and foremost."

"Why?"

"Well, because..."

"Inter-Allied is not an American Regiment. God knows what we are. American? British? Lunar Colony? You can't even stop at human, as we aren't all that."

"Okay, how do you want me to proceed?"

"You take the best recruits you can find. I don't care what ship they come from. I don't care if they're men, women, black, or white. It doesn't matter. You just make sure they're the best, you hear?"

"Okay."

"I'm not even sure our name Inter-Allied even means anything anymore. It was merely to symbolize the unity between two nations."

"Then go by our other name."

Taylor stopped and looked at her in surprise. "What do you mean?"

"The Immortals?"

Taylor thought about it for a moment.

"We're a mix of outfits from different nations, and it is your choice to make now. The name served us well, and there isn't a soul in this fleet that doesn't know the name."

"We are ultimately all marines now, by definition of what we do aboard this fleet. But I don't want to rob those other units of their heritage. Immortals it is."

"The Immortal Regiment? Parker asked, "Sounds good."

Taylor laughed. "Well, good, I wouldn't want us to sound anything unimportant."

They reached the quarters of the recruits. It was familiar, as it was the exact same layout and design as their own. He stopped in the doorway and turned to Parker.

"Everything we got," said Taylor, "it's not exactly tough conditions to get them motivated."

"You're assuming that we lead a life of luxury," replied Parker.

"True."

"And it's not like I can have them out in the wilderness, slogging through the mud and sleeping in dugouts. If only."

"So we're gonna have to find new ways to toughen them up. What sort of backgrounds have they got?"

"I tried to focus on anyone with prior experience that might help. A few have been in the Corps. We've got ex-cops, private security, doormen, and gym instructors. Had to take what I could get."

One of the recruits closer to the door finally noticed them and called out.

"Attention on deck!"

Many of them almost jumped out of their skin and tried to get up and look presentable. Not one of them had a uniform. They wore their own civilian clothing.

"As you were!" Taylor yelled.

He didn't want to address them as a unit. He wanted to see them individually and to look into their eyes; see what kind of people they were. He passed down the line of beds slowly, looking at every single one of them, and studying every little detail. He looked at the photos of loved ones they had pinned to the beds and jewellery hanging from the hooks. It was clear to him from the clothing, they were from every social standing that could be thought of. But he didn't say a word to any of them, not until he reached a familiar face.

"Mia Moore," he said.

She was lying casually in her bed on top of the sheets, wearing nothing more than her underwear and a tight fitting black t-shirt. She looked provocative, and yet like she was ready to pounce and rip someone's throat out at a moment's notice.

"Not afraid one of these fine specimens will try and jump you with a look like that?" he asked her.

She gestured over to the bunk opposite. Taylor looked over to see a well-built man in his late twenties. He had a black eye and was nursing a damaged ego. Taylor laughed.

"What's your name, Son?"

"Adrian Hill, Sir."

"You learnt a valuable lesson here. Or at least, I hope you did."

"Yes, Sir?"

"Never underestimate your opponent. You saw a cute girl. What you didn't see was the lion inside that girl. Don't ever make such a dumb mistake again. In here, it cost you a black eye. In combat, it could cost you your life, but more important than that, the lives of your fellow marines."

"Yes, Sir," he said solemnly.

"And don't be ashamed. You feel your ego has been knocked because someone half your size did this to you? You gotta start thinking outside the box. If you thought she was no trouble because of her size, how will you feel when you face an alien twice your size?"

Taylor could see almost hear the cogs turning in the man's brain as he realized what Taylor was saying.

"Thank you, Sir."

Two days passed while Taylor oversaw their training. It was half way through the third day. The recruits carried dummy training rifles and were practicing gaining and giving ground, with obstacles setup through the gymnasium for them to navigate. His arms were crossed, and he watched from afar, as Parker made them practice the same drill for the twelfth time that day. She shouted at them every few seconds as they made mistakes, but he was glad to see their progress was at least respectable.

It felt just like old times, back on Earth and observing the grilling of a new set of hopefuls. The only difference being that an alien, Jafar, stood at his side. Then the last thing he ever would have expected happened. Admiral Huber came over the intercom on an open channel to the fleet.

"This is Admiral Huber speaking."

Everyone stopped what they were doing and listened.

"One hour ago, I received word from the frigate, the Valentine, one of the six vessels that departed almost three days ago to search out this system and discover our surroundings. Above all, their mission was to find a habitable planet that we might make our own, a planet where humanity may rebuild and start over. I am here to tell you that the crew of the Valentine has found that planet."

Taylor couldn't believe what he was hearing, and yet he looked across the room to see the others had heard just the same. First there was a stunned silence, and then the recruits began throwing their arms up in the air in joy, whistling and shouting in excitement. Parker looked to him with a new sense of hope, but he was not sold on the news at all. He turned to Jafar, who looked emotionless, as he often did.

"Did you know there was such a planet in this system?"

"I did not," he replied quickly, "but I know very little of this system. Is that not good news?"

"It might be. But it stinks. We've never found a habitable planet in all the years humanity has been in space."

"That is not very long, is it?"

"Well, no, but still. Don't you think it's just a little convenient that we lose our planet, jump to somewhere random, and bam, there's one here for us?"

"This was not a random choice."

"No, that's true, and that worries me even more."

Taylor was the only one not celebrating. He turned to leave.

"Jafar, on me!"

He stormed up to the bridge. Every crewmember he passed was beaming with excitement, and idle chitchat filled the corridors of the carrier, but he was not falling for it. He reached the bridge and found the same level of ecstasy. Huber was grinning from ear to ear.

"Colonel Taylor, your plan worked. None of us could have expected it quite so soon, but we've done it. We've found a new home!"

"What do we know about the planet? Are there any signs of life? Any sign of Krys presence?"

Huber backed off, looked at Taylor's stern expression, and finally laughed.

"Colonel Taylor. After all we have been through, this is a victory, and should be celebrated as such. Don't you know what this means?"

"No, not yet, none of us do."

He leaned in closer to the Admiral.

"Sir, I must recommend we proceed with the utmost caution. Every action we make risks the entire fleet. I would not have us gamble it all on this planet, without a thorough investigation first."

"Yes, yes of course. We aren't putting down there with everything we have. I am arranging an expeditionary force, as well as a team of scientists and experts to head there right away and assess the situation."

"If I may, Sir? If boots are going on the ground, then I should be among them, and so should Jafar. Beyond the science, we are your best bet at making sure the place is safe."

Huber's face turned more serious.

"I have no doubt you are, Colonel, but your job is to maintain the safety and security of this vessel, and therefore this fleet."

"I am attempting to do that, Sir."

"Damn you, Taylor, enough of this nonsense. This is a time to celebrate, and I have plenty of work for you yet. The number of casualties three days ago was completely unacceptable. Your job is to investigate why it went wrong and find solutions so that it does not happen again."

"Sir, I must protest."

"No, you most certainly must not. You're a good man and a damn fine officer, Taylor, but right now I don't need your cynical outlook. I need your expertise where it is needed most. I want you working closely with Reiter and his team to workout whatever you need to handle those Juggernauts, as you call them. God forbid we ever have to face them again."

We? It wasn't you who had to face them.

But he didn't dare say it out loud.

"You are dismissed, Taylor. And Colonel? Try to look on the bright side. A little history is being made here."

Taylor turned and left.

"That's what worries me," he whispered to himself.

The jubilation of every soul aboard the ship was intoxicating. He wondered if he was the only one among them who saw the potential danger they were in.

"What do we do?" Jafar asked.

Taylor wasn't sure whether he meant figuratively or literally, but it didn't matter.

"What we've been ordered to."

CHAPTER ELEVEN

Taylor stood before the armoured suit of a Juggernaut. It was suspended from a hoist normally used for the engines of aircraft. A pool of blood lay on the deck beneath it, expanding as the thick blue substance still dripped from the armour. It was clear the creature's corpse was still inside. He couldn't help but just stand and stare at it. He'd never gotten the opportunity to actually look at the details.

In combat, all Taylor saw was a figure as he focused on the centre body mass and used peripheral vision. To him the Juggernaut was just a larger Mech suit. But now up close, he could see it was something quite different. Its leg joints were set differently, and there appeared to be no power source for the suit like the normal Mech models.

"What is it?" he asked Jafar who stood beside him.

"I believe it is a Boga."

"A what?"

"A primitive creature. Much like your apes are to humans. They share some genetic material and evolutionary path with my kind, but they are crude and simple."

"But big and strong."

"Yes, far stronger than we are, but they are wild animals."

"Don't look wild to me. They are armoured and came at us in a determined fashion. How do you explain that?"

"I cannot."

"Modules attached to the brain," Reiter said, walking past behind them.

He stopped between the two of them and looked at the armour with the same fascination Taylor had been doing.

"Yes, the creature itself is a rather primitive beast, but clad in this armour and with a simple control algorithm."

"What algorithm?"

"Very simple really. The Mech armours transmit identification for friendly forces through sound. These Juggernauts are programmed to attack and kill any living creature that does not emit their code, and is punished by electric shocks if they step within a metre of one who does."

"So they're little more than a crazed beast they let loose to raise hell?"

"As you like," replied Reiter.

Taylor moved along to the next creature suspended from another crane. Its arm was severed and hanging from a chain beside it. He could see it was the one he and

Jafar had taken down together.

"They are formidable things, these Boga, or whatever they are. In open ground, where we could bring heavier weapons to bear, they wouldn't be so much an issue. But aboard these ships in the corridors and confines, they're like bulls in a china shop, and we're the china."

He turned and looked at Reiter.

"What answer have you got to this problem? How can we take them down?"

Reiter shook his head. "I am not sure yet. I need your ideas. You have fought them."

"Yes, we have, and we paid for it dearly."

"I am working on ideas, Colonel, but you are the soldier, not I."

"Marine."

"Yes, that, too."

Taylor looked back to the creatures.

"Their armour? It's far thicker than anything we have had to deal with. The Reitech ammo barely touches it."

"It is nothing technologically impressive. It is the same armour the soldiers wear, but three times the thickness. They are like walking armoured vehicles."

"Then maybe that is the answer. Stop treating them like infantry, and start treating them like tanks. Maybe it is that simple. Their armour is three times thicker. Fine, we just need weapons that pack three times the punch?"

"Easier said than done, Colonel. Those weapons

are already formidable pieces of hardware. If I were to increase the calibre and power of the ammunition used, the equivalent weapon would be so large you would likely not even be able to lift it. They would in fact be just like some of the Reitech vehicular mounted devices."

"That sounds good."

"You don't understand me, Colonel. The weapons I developed far outweigh anything used in the past. The rifles you carry today are of an equivalent weight to heavy machine guns of by gone years. They are…come with me."

He led them around some containers to an armaments rack for the fighter and support craft of the Washington. He pointed at a gun that was two metres long, and resembled little more than a thick pipe with a box receiver and feed for ammunition.

"That is the kind of weapon you speak of. Lift it."

Taylor looked at him as if he were a fool.

"Go on, try and lift it. With your suit on," he said, pointing to a rack of the exo-skeletons opposite.

He climbed into the suit and then confidently walked up to the rack of weaponry. Never before had he struggled with strength in his suit, so he did not doubt its abilities.

"The Reitech 50CMG, commonly fitted with coaxial weapons on main battle tanks and as close support and ground attack craft. A marvel, I might add. Now try and lift it," said Reiter.

Taylor stepped up to the rack and got a solid grip on the weapon before hauling it upwards in a deadlift fashion. He strained to do so and got upright with it in his hands. He tried to raise it and turn his body as if to aim it, but felt his body shake. It was the feeling of weakness he had all but forgotten. He clumsily lowered it back down, and it slammed into the rack and echoed out across the hangar bay.

"I can't use that!" he yelled.

Reiter nodded. "As I said. The 50CMG weighs almost four hundred kilograms. Even with the power of your suit, it is unusable in a combat situation in any manner, except a fixed point on a vehicle or emplacement."

"That's no good to me, Doc. I need something we can use on the move. Have you nothing else?"

"Give me time, Colonel. I understand your requirements. Though I'm not sure how much more portable I can make the kind of weapon you require."

"Just do what you can, Doc."

Taylor pulled off the armour and strode off with Jafar at his side.

"Those things are sons of a bitches. We need to find a better way to take them out. You got any ideas?"

"I fight with the weapons I am given. I am not an engineer."

"Yeah, well join the club."

* * *

"Okay, people, this is our biggest one yet," said Kelly.

He looked out across the operations table and they all looked to him. Twenty personnel, including all of the key officers involved.

"Every single day a convoy of vehicles travels back and forth along this road," he said, as he pointed to a map.

"That is, twelve vehicles in total."

"These are wheeled vehicles?" Oster asked.

"Yes."

"Why are they using wheeled vehicles when they have so many aircraft?"

"You got me. If we understood everything they did, then perhaps we wouldn't be in the situation we are in today. We know they used land-based vehicles throughout the war. They were far more susceptible to our heavy guns, and maybe that's why we didn't see so many of them back then. But they think they've won. They think they own this country now. Own this world. So they're moving freely without worry. Maybe they are cutting costs by travelling by road, or maybe they're staying under the radar of remaining Earth air forces."

"Yeah, right. Can't be any left," replied Oster.

"I can speculate till the World ends, and you can be a cynical idiot till that time, too, but it isn't going to get the job done."

Oster didn't say another word.

"Okay, so here's how it's gonna happen. We know the route they take, and we know roughly the time they make it each day. During the night, we are going to move four of the main battle tanks into dugout hull down positions overlooking the road here, and here. That will have to be done in complete blackout conditions. You okay with that, Captain?" he asked Becker.

"Shouldn't be a problem. We start early at sundown so we can let the engines tick over most of the way. We shouldn't attract any attention."

"Okay, the plan is simple. The road at this point crosses from one side of the valley to the other. That's half a klick. We position two tanks in well-concealed positions at either side of the valley and near the roadside. Additionally, we establish trenches with fifty men here, and another twenty in reserve here," he said, pointing to the map.

"It certainly is a simple plan, think it can work?" Decker asked.

"I wouldn't suggest it if I didn't think so."

"Remember," Kelly said, "The three priorities here in order are, maintain the safety of this facility, get back alive, and kill the enemy. Those are your priorities at all times. If we have to abandon those tanks, we do so. If we have to kill the wounded, or else have them captured by the enemy, we do so. Do you all understand?"

It was a grim outlook, but they agreed anyway.

"All right then, we move at nightfall. Dismissed."

The group split up, and only Becker remained sitting opposite Kelly.

"So this is it, first big one?"

"No," said Kelly, "Merely an escalation of what we have already been doing. And you'd do well to ensure your people know that, or else they'll have doubts as to our success."

"And do you not have doubts?"

"Of course I have doubts. If I did not, I would either be foolish or insane."

"Do we have any idea what is aboard those vehicles?"

"No, and we have no way of doing so. Except to track them to their source. And I have no desire to go anywhere near the cities or their bases. Are you okay with this plan? You can back out or question it at any time."

Becker took a deep breath and thought about it for a moment.

"No, I am as confident as I can be."

Becker pulled out a hip flask and took a drink before passing it over to Kelly.

"No, not tonight. Not until I have seen this through."

Becker didn't mind and took the drink for him.

"Okay. I'll see you in a few hours," he said as he got up and left. Kelly swivelled around in his chair to see Reynolds waiting at the door for him.

"Something you want to talk about, Captain?"

"Not really."

"Then what can I do for you?"

"Just be yourself, Sir. We have a few hours before all this kicks off, can we not get a coffee and chat like it were old times?"

Kelly smiled and nodded. "Of course."

He would say anything to calm the nerves of his people, but this time he actually welcomed the proposal to sit with old friends before it all began. They headed for the canteen where they found over a hundred personnel sat about socialising. They took a seat and soon found Corporal Berlin heading for them.

"May I sit with you, Sir?"

"You don't need to ask. The old rank structure is not what it was. I lead because I am good at it, but not for any other reason. You treat me as your equal."

It was clear she didn't see his point of view and responded, "Thank you, Sir." She sat down opposite him.

"What can I do for you, Corporal…"

"Berlin, Sir."

"I know that is your family name. But what is the name you choose to go by, what do your friends call you?" he asked.

"My name is Letta, Sir, and that is what they call me."

"And am I a friend? Would you have me call you Letta?"

"If that is your preference, Sir."

Kelly shook his head. He opened his mouth to respond

but decided he wasn't going to get anywhere and stopped.

"Sir, what I wanted to ask you is what many here are asking. What are you doing in Germany? You are colonists of the Moon. Why come to Germany?"

Kelly laughed. "It wasn't by choice, I can tell you. Not that I had anything against the country, but I knew little of Earth, except for what I learnt at school. We were placed here by the UEN. They chose the spot. We just went where they told us."

"And that was okay with you?"

"Why wouldn't it be? You are born some place that isn't of your choosing and you learn to get on with it, and hopefully like it. So we got another place that wasn't of our choosing, and we got on fine here, too. I'd certainly appreciate a warmer climate in winter, but beggars can't be choosers."

* * *

A day had passed and Taylor and Jafar stood before Reiter once again.

"One day, Taylor? One day? Do you know how long it takes to develop an idea and experiment and trial? I've barely begun to draw up some ideas."

"Come on, Doc, you work fast. You're famous for it. We need a solution; you must have a few ideas. Throw them at us."

He shook his head, muttering under his breath, but went over to a display console and activated it so that a projection displayed before them.

"I have thoroughly tested the 50CMG against these new armours and have come to the conclusion that they possess the appropriate operational requirements."

"No shit, Doc, they're fucking cannons. That ain't the problem."

"No," he replied, "We have the right weapon. I cannot at present substantially reduce the weight of the weapon, without compromising its effectiveness. And so we are left with just one choice; to find diverse ways of making it operationally viable to men and women like yourself in the field."

"Okay," Taylor replied. He sounded suspicious, "But we already decided it isn't viable to use as a personal weapon in combat."

"No, it is not. So then we must surely stop looking for complicated solutions to our problem, and start looking to far more primitive and proven ones."

"A retrograde step?"

"Not exactly, Colonel. Think of the weapon you carry on your side that you now know as your Assegai. It is a useful weapon in combat, yes?"

He nodded. "More than useful."

"And yet for all the technological marvel contained in that weapon, it is for all intents and purposes little more than a sword or small spear, is it not?"

"Yes, Doc, but come on; stop talking in riddles."

"Riddles? This is no riddle. I am merely trying to make your simple minds understand some simple logic."

Taylor looked carefully at the plans projected before him. The principal image showed a simple metal tripod with the gun mounted atop it.

"What is this primitive crap?"

"A tripod. A simple device yes, but one that enables the use of heavy weapons by mobile infantry forces in the field. This is not my invention. It is nothing new or revolutionary. But why reinvent the wheel? You need the ability to take heavy ordnance into combat by foot. Using a three-weapon fireteam, where two men carry the weapon from shoulder to shoulder and another carries the tripod, you have your solution."

Taylor rubbed his chin as he thought it over.

"There are surely other ways to solve your problem, but they will take time, and resources we may not even have. This method will enable you to make use of current weaponry. Tripods are an elegantly simple solution to a big problem. I can have a handful of prototypes built within a day, and full production within a week. It requires nothing more than steel and simple machinery.

"This is your answer? You have nothing more?"

"Overall, I think this is the best solution to your problem. However, I am working on a revision to your shields that would enable them to be used as rests for the 50CMG and allow quick deployment in close quarter battle."

"Go on."

He walked across the room to where a shield lay clamped in a work unit. At the top, a section had been cut out in a U shape, approximately thirty centimetres wide and deep.

"This simple modification will allow the wielder to deploy a rest for the 50CMG that will make it immediately combat effective."

Taylor laughed. "A shield with a barrel shape cut in the top? Doc you really are working on some primitive levels here."

"Yes I am, Colonel. Time is of the essence, more important than anything else. I want you to have a useable means of operating these weapons and defeating these hideous monsters before you have to face them again. You keep us all alive, protect us all, Colonel. I am well aware of that fact. I would not recommend second-rate equipment. This is my recommendation to get the best kit into the field as quickly as is possible."

Taylor nodded his head, thinking about it a little longer. He thought of the Juggernauts and how vicious they were. He remembered how much he would give to have had an effective way to take them down.

"Do it," he stated.

"You are sure you want to proceed? You have not sounded too keen, Colonel?"

"If this is the only way we can get it done right now, then very well. I want three of your tripods and three of these modified shields by morning, can you do that?"

"I believe so."

"Then do it, and we shall find out if your old ideas still work in today's war."

* * *

Once again Kelly found he was in a dug out. The snow had begun to settle, and the temperatures seemed to be dropping every day. He had sat there for hours and was starting to feel numb.

"We've been here for too long, Kelly. This doesn't feel right," said Becker.

The Captain sat next to him.

"I'm surprised you aren't in one of those tanks," he replied.

"I command tank platoons, but now I must do it from here. Would I rather be in a comfy commander's seat than slumming it our here with you? Damn right I would."

"And yet here you are."

"Don't rub it in."

"Here they come!" Berlin shouted.

They grabbed their rifles and took up positions. Kelly

raised his rifle to use the scope to look ahead for the enemy. They could see nothing beyond the thick tree line. It was their greatest asset in almost every situation. But now he could feel his heart pounding as he waited for the enemy to come into view. He told himself they knew what was coming because they had observed it for days, but he also knew there was plenty of room for variables they did not understand. He tried with all his will to slow his breathing and calm his heart rate.

The first vehicle finally rolled into view. It was a six-wheeled vehicle that was fully enclosed. It looked of heavyweight construction but without substantial ammo to its payload.

'What do you think they're carrying?" Becker asked.

"Who knows? Looks like your average transport, maybe some kind of fuel or ammunition. But they seem to move everything by air. The only land vehicles we see are heavy tanks and the like."

"What are you saying?"

"That I don't like this."

"What do you mean, we're seconds away from hitting these fuckers?"

"Think about it, Captain. We barely ever see a land vehicle, and then we start seeing them on a set schedule and route within twenty klicks of where we have been hitting them?"

"Why are you questioning this now when we're just

about to hit them?"

"But I'm not sure. I'm not sure this is safe."

"Too late, Kelly. We came here to waste these sons of bitches, and we're gonna do it. We're seconds away from sending them to hell!"

Becker raised his rifle and took aim at the lead vehicle. He knew he probably couldn't damage the armour, but it was the signal for his tank crews to engage the enemy.

"Becker, no, you could kill us all!" Kelly pleaded.

It was too late. Becker squeezed the trigger, and two shots glanced off the lead vehicle.

Oh, God! Kelly thought.

A moment later they heard the thunder of two of the tanks opening fire, and the lead enemy truck ignited into a ball of flames. It veered off the road and crashed into an embankment.

"Yeah!" Becker shouted.

They watched in horror as a dozen Mechs spilled out of the burning wreck and came out shooting. Becker ducked back down for cover as pulses smashed into their position.

"I told you not to do this!"

"This was your mission, Kelly!"

Kelly couldn't think of any words to say as he ducked back in the trench for cover. Finally, he decided he had no choice now but to get up and join in the battle. He put his rifle on the edge of the trench and took aim at the nearest Mech. He fired two shots that met their target, but ducked down as pulses smashed into the top of the trench where he had been moments before.

As the fire settled down, he looked back over the trench. Their tanks continued to fire and strike the vehicles in the column, but he could see more than thirty Mechs advancing up the hill to their position.

"We can't stay here!"

"We have to complete the mission!"

"No, Captain, we have to survive to fight another day!"

They heard an explosion and looked over the embankment. One of their tanks was engulfed in flames, and they all knew the crew could not have survived. A moment later, three pulses struck their position from a fighter strafing them, and Kelly saw at least a few of their people be engulfed in their fire.

"Goddamn it!" Becker swore and slumped back down into the trench, throwing down is rifle, 'This is fucked!"

"Yes it is!" Kelly replied, "It is, and remember out strategy. We are compromised, so let's get the hell out of here!"

As he said it, a fighter strafed their position, and they ducked down for cover. Pulses smashed into their position, and Kelly felt the burn of fragments from one of them embed in his shoulder. He cried out in pain but told himself it wasn't there. He knew whatever injury he had must wait.

Kelly climbed up to the edge of the trench and could

see another of their tanks was burning now, and more than fifty Mechs were approaching up the hill.

"If we stay here, we die!"

"I won't leave my people!" Becker screamed.

Kelly smacked him across the jaw, which hurt him as much as Becker.

"They die whether we go or not," he added, cradling his shoulder and wincing in pain.

Becker didn't know how to respond. He looked to Berlin who was the only soldier he seemed to trust.

"We have to go, Sir. We fight at a place and time of our choosing. This is their ambush, their time. We stay here and we lose."

Becker shook his head. "Our greatest fucking victory is actually our greatest fucking embarrassment. Go!"

Berlin grabbed Kelly and hauled him out of the trench while Becker relayed the command across the comms. Breaking radio silence was a last resort, and Kelly at least appreciated that Becker was now taking the situation seriously. They rushed out of the trench and back down the other side of the hill giving them cover from the advancing enemy. Fifty metres of running, and they reached the line of vehicles they had positioned for their return journey. They never expected them to be needed so soon. Kelly climbed into the driving seat of his truck.

"You think you can drive with that shoulder?" Berlin asked.

"I can drive a lot better than I can I can hold a rifle, right now."

She understood and climbed into the back of the vehicle. He fired up the engine as Becker leapt aboard, and he put his foot to the floor. The wheels spun as the vehicle roared forward, and those behind them quickly followed suit.

They tore through the forest road at a rapid rate, and it wasn't long before they saw enemy vessels overhead tracking their position. They fired randomly through the canopy of the forest but could not accurately pinpoint the location of the vehicles.

"Get on that gun!" Kelly hollered.

Berlin was quick to respond and climbed into the seat of the anti-aircraft gun that had been reinstalled on his vehicle.

'It's fucked," Becker said, "It's all fucked."

Berlin ignored him and squeezed the trigger on the guns. Their roar was deafening as shots pierced the canopy and riddled the enemy vessels with fire. The first blew and scattered into flaming pieces as the others broke off their pursuit. She finally took her finger of the trigger and looked back to Becker. He was a mess.

"Kelly, stop the truck!" he yelled, "Stop the truck!"

Kelly hit the brakes, and the vehicle slid to a halt. The others in the convoy were forced to do the same. He got out and stood beside the bed. He saw that Becker couldn't even move through the shock.

"We have to go back. Those are my people," he cried.

"Remember what I told you, Captain. The individual counts for nothing. They must make their own way home now, or not at all."

Becker shook his head. "And if those were your people out there? What about you? What if it was you we left out there?"

"Then I'd expect you to put a bullet in my head before you left, to ensure I told the enemy nothing."

Becker nodded in agreement. He knew it was the case, but it was still painful to accept.

"They saw our every move here, Kelly," he finally said.

"Yes they did, and all that means is we have to be smarter. We have to predict their next move."

"And if we can't?"

"What do you mean can't? We can do whatever we put our minds to. Even better, we can outthink them, and do you know why?"

Becker shook his head.

"Because they aren't that smart."

It brought a smile to Becker's face, and that was enough. Kelly climbed back into the driver's seat and continued on.

CHAPTER TWELVE

Five days later.

"Colonel Taylor to the bridge. Colonel Taylor to the bridge."

Ah, great, he thought.

"Looks like they're after your ass once again," Parker said.

"Aren't they always?" he jested.

He headed right for the bridge, and Jafar was with him as usual. It was hard to shake the alien.

"Don't you ever have something you want to do on your own?" Taylor asked as they approached the bridge.

"What is there to do?" he asked, "I live to fight. There is no one to fight, so I serve my duty of protecting you."

"And that doesn't ever bore you?"

He shook his head.

They reached the bridge to find Huber nowhere to be

seen.

"Captain Vega, where is the Admiral?"

"He has requested your presence in his private quarters, Colonel. Just you!" Vega emphasised.

He carried on without Jafar and stepped through into Huber's quarters. He found him slumped at his desk. He looked troubled and exhausted; far from the figure of joy and celebration he had been upon news of the planet discovery.

"What can I do for you, Sir?"

"Taylor. When we found this planet, the only person in the whole damn fleet that was sceptical about it was you. I thought you a fool."

"What is the problem, Sir?"

"Nothing as imminent as an enemy with a rifle, but so many small problems that are mounting to make me... uncomfortable. Perhaps you tempted fate."

"I don't believe in fate, Admiral. That would suggest someone else is pulling my strings, and I don't accept that."

"Is that why you have such a problem with authority?"

"Perhaps, but I have never done anything that is not in the best interests of us all."

"Or what you perceive is our best interests?"

"I can only work on my gut."

Huber smiled. "If it were anyone else, you'd be in long-term stay in my brig, Taylor. And yet no bars seem to hold you back, and no man can ever fully command you. But

I will not make the mistake of locking horns with you, as so many before me have. As Admiral of the fleet, I must make use of every asset at my disposal. You're not perfect, Colonel, but you are invaluable."

"Thank you, Sir."

Huber went silent and slipped back into deep thought. Taylor could not help but feel the situation was bizarre.

"Sir?"

He looked up, seemingly surprised and waited for a question.

"The planetary issues you mentioned?"

He nodded, taking a drink of water from the glass beside him and wiping his tired eyes.

"It is not one big problem, more a collection of a great many smaller ones."

"What do you mean, Sir?"

He picked up a tablet device and started scrolling through a list.

"I've got reports of engine failures, sickness among various members of both the civilians and military personnel down there. Sightings of strange things in the nights, screams from marines who say they saw ghosts or dreamed of their death; heavy storms that are destroying equipment. Whatever is going on down there, it's a mess, and a mess I want you to clear up. It's almost as if the planet itself doesn't want us to step foot there."

"Sounds crazy, Sir?"

"Yes it does. But for whatever the reasons are for all this nonsense, I will not risk any substantial deployment until I know what we're dealing with, and why. This may just be a case of fear and uncertainty playing tricks on the mind. There may be a perfectly reasonable answer to it, but I want to know for certain."

"I'll get right on it, Sir."

"Yes, good. And be sure to take your own air supply. Do not breath the air. Do not drink the water or make physical contact with any object. People are going crazy down there, and I don't want you following them."

"What kind of deployment would you have me make?"

"You take enough that you can deal with any kind of trouble that might arise, but not so much you leave this ship undefended."

Great, deliberately vague.

"I'll take a hundred of my people. That will leave you with more than enough, Admiral."

He nodded and waved as if to accept whatever Taylor had to say. Mitch turned to leave when the Admiral made one last passing comment.

"This is a problem I don't need, Taylor. Do whatever you have to do."

Taylor carried on without another word. He found Jafar waiting at the door, with two of the Admiral's guards standing uneasily in front of him.

"Looks like we finally got some real work to do."

"Who do we have to kill?" Jafar asked.

Taylor patted him on the back.

"Nobody I know of, but who knows? You might have an opportunity yet."

An hour later, he stood before the hundred of his own unit that had been assembled. Lieutenants Matthews and Anders, as well as Parker. Three platoons awaited his orders, and Morris stood beside him, knowing nothing more than any other of them.

"You all know by now that we have discovered a planet our experts believe is habitable," he began, "For now we are calling this newly discovered world Atlantis. A fitting name for such a remarkable discovery, if it is indeed what we believe it is."

Many of them seem surprised by his scepticism.

"Don't get me wrong. I want this planet to be all we hoped it to be, but let's not get ahead of ourselves. The Admiral has had marines and teams of experts on the surface for several days now. They have as yet not met any resistance or enemy presence, but there are many unexplained occurrences that are making people uneasy and scared. We are going there to resolve whatever we have to. I don't know yet what that will mean, but as ever, we improvise and overcome. Any questions?"

No one said a word.

"Lastly, the 50CMG, you have all now trained on it, and we have one per platoon. Tripods will be issued, as well as the modified shields for fireteams."

"Sir?" Watkins asked.

"Yes, Private, what is it?"

"Are you really expecting us to lug those lumps of pig iron about?"

"You're damn right I am. They're big old beasts, but they also pack a hell of a punch. Next time we come up against some heavy armour, I want to see you punching holes in it, you hear?"

"Yes, Sir."

"Now, Reiter has reduced the weight and size of our 50CMG as much as is possible. We've got shortened barrels and reduced heat shielding. We'll lose a little of the range and accuracy over distance, and they won't stand up to sustained fire over prolonged periods. But they'll at least be a little easier for you to lug about and get into action. Pig iron? I like that. They are a pig to lug about, and that's what we'll call them. Any more questions?"

"What are our intentions when we reach the surface, Sir?" asked Parker, "What are we aiming to achieve?"

Taylor shrugged. "At present, I just don't know enough to say. What I can guarantee is that from what Huber tells me, it is one big cluster fuck. So we'll have to deal with the situation as it unfolds."

"But what is our purpose? Are we there to fight, as security, or what?"

Taylor shrugged once again. "No idea, Matthews,

that's for us to find out. You can keep framing the same questions in new ways, but the simple fact is, I don't know any more than I have already told you."

In actual fact, he did, but he didn't want to spook them. The last thing he wanted was for his own people to be infected with the same hysteria he had heard about before they even reached the planet. He wanted them to form their own conclusions, based on their own experiences.

"Well, okay then, load up and move out!"

He watched as Watkins and Abbot headed for the 50CMG and hauled it onto their shoulders. May followed after them with the tripod. It was a clumsy piece of equipment, but he like the thought of having some big guns at his side.

"Really are a pig," muttered Abbot.

Taylor strode aboard the Mercury that awaited him and noted the name on the side, 'Gerty'. He could see from the repairs it was indeed the same ship they had been in for the mission to the space gateway that nearly ended in their deaths. As he stepped inside, he found Rains already in the pilot's seat.

"You got her going again?"

"Yes, Sir, the old girl is back."

"Don't you think the fact she almost killed us first time out is reason enough to leave her on the bench?"

"What are you talking about, Colonel? How many died on that mission?"

"None."

"And how many wounded?"

"None."

"So what you're saying is she got us all home safe and sound, and she was the only one that got hurt? Sounds like our guardian angel to me."

Taylor shook his head.

"You're a funny son of a bitch, you know that?"

"Hell, yes I do. You gotta keep smiling, Colonel. Enjoy life while we still have it."

It wasn't long before they were lifting off, and even sooner, they were landing aboard the Valentine. It was almost two days' journey to Atlantis. Taylor's first glance at the planet was through the cockpit of Gerty. Oceans spanned almost half the world. That alone made it inviting to the human eye.

"Looks familiar, doesn't it?" Rains asked.

He was right. It did look a lot like Earth from afar. But as they passed through the atmosphere, they could see much of the surface was dry craggy land.

"Is that..." started Rains.

They were looking at the layout of a city, and yet only remnants of the foundations remained that told them so.

"A city? Looks like it was a hell of a long time ago."

"So something lived here?"

"Or still does," replied Taylor.

They put down half a kilometre south of the edge of

the old city where they found a compound that had been built by the first teams to reach the planet. Nobody came to greet them as they landed, but they could see various personnel about the site. Taylor was first out and looked up at the sky and at the ground all around him. It was not unlike parts of North Africa where he had fought Demiran. He could feel the heat rising from the ground. The rays of light from the sun were so strong; he could feel his eyes stinging from the intensity. He immediately activated the UV filter and dimmed the mask of his helmet.

"Doesn't look half bad," said Parker.

"And yet none of them look to happy to be here," added Lieutenant Anders.

Taylor looked to Jafar for information, but it was clear he had none. He looked up to a guard tower overlooking their landing zone. Even from afar, he could see the body language of the woman on duty. She looked lost and sick. It was a look of loss he would expect to see in a soldier after days of brutal combat.

"What aren't you telling us, Mitch?"

"All I know, Eli, is some strange shit is going down here, and it's our job to find out what."

"So what now?"

"You are to stay on base, Anders, and investigate here. Talk to whoever is in charge, talk to anyone who will do so. Find out whatever you can."

"I am no detective."

"No, you're a problem solver with a gun. Get to it. The rest of us are heading into the remnants of that city. I figure whatever is going on here, it's probably got something to do with that place."

"But what is going on here?"

He ignored Parker's question.

"Anders, you have your orders. Everyone else, on me."

He carried on walking right out of the base without a word to anyone in it.

"I don't like this at all," said Parker, "We're just wandering around with absolutely no idea what we're doing. What was really our purpose of coming here?"

"The Admiral didn't say it. But I believe he is concerned a force is at work here that threatens our plans for colonisation."

"Force? What force? All I have seen is a few pissed off and bored marines. There's nothing new there."

They carried on across the open plain towards the remains of the city ahead. It was a bizarre experience. Taylor almost felt as if was in a dream. It was almost like Earth, but he knew it wasn't.

"Sir?"

"Go on, Watkins."

"Well, Sir, it's like this. The aliens came to Earth because they wanted our planet, right?"

"Yeah, so I'm told."

"But this one seems pretty good to me. Why did they

fight us for ours when they could have had this one, no trouble?"

Taylor grimaced. It made him think of all kinds of possibilities in his head, and none of them were good.

"Jafar, you said your people call this death space, or whatever. You want to shed some light on that? It could well explain the Private's concerns."

"All that I know have told you. The Krys know that those who venture here do not return."

"The implication that something dwells here that doesn't like you too much?"

"Yes."

"And you thought that being human we'd just be okay?" Watkins asked.

"It was a logical gamble, as you say."

Watkins suddenly tripped and stumbled, dropping the barrel of the pig as he tumbled rather ungraciously into the dirt.

"What the hell?" he asked.

He got up and went back to the gun. He noticed something metallic sticking out from the ground that he had kicked and scraped. Taylor had seen it, too, as the sun glinted off the surface it had revealed.

"Well that's not natural."

Watkins knelt down beside it and scraped away the sand and dirt off it as the others looked on. He stopped when he revealed the shape of a metallic hand and forearm.

"Krys..." said Taylor.

Several of them were spooked and looked around half expecting trouble to come their way, but nothing happened. Jafar knelt down, got a hold of the object, and pulled it out from the ground. It was just the gauntlet and forearm from Mech armour. There was no sign of living remains inside. Jafar looked at it curiously and with suspicion.

"What is it?" Taylor asked.

"This armour, it is Krys, but old, and maybe five hundred of your years. I have only seen such armours used for the guards of honour to the Lords of Worlds."

"How long do you think it's been here?"

"Some time at least."

"What does that mean?"

"Right now, Watkins, it means shit," replied Taylor.

He looked to Jafar.

"You've really told us everything you know of this place?"

"Until now I did not know of the existence of this planet."

That was enough for Taylor. He carried on and followed what loosely resembled a road into the city. The surface had long been covered over with sand and dirt and not a single wall over a metre tall still stood.

"What do you think happened here?"

"I'd say someone went all out and flattened it, Parker."

It made sense, but it was just a guess. They paced through

272

the ruins, looking for a sign of anything. Something that might tell them who and what lived there, and what had caused their destruction. Taylor suddenly noticed a small buzzing noise behind him. He turned to see a tiny flying object, not more than a couple of centimetres wide floating before him. It glinted in the sun and appeared to be mechanical. There was distortion all around it by what appeared to be the motion of wings or fans.

"What the hell is that?" Parker asked, raising her rifle at the ready.

It floated right in front of Taylor as if it were studying him.

"Is that...a machine?"

"Looks like it, Parker. Nobody move. Whatever it is, we give it no reason to react."

"Come on, Colonel, it's a fucking insect!" Abbot laughed.

"We don't know what it is or isn't, but it is certainly curious about us. My guess is it's some kind of drone."

"So someone is controlling it?" Parker asked.

It turned away from Taylor and flew around the group, as if checking and logging every one of them.

"Maybe, or at least someone monitoring whatever it sees."

"What do we do?"

"Nothing until we have reason to do so, Parker."

Finally, the bug-like object reached Jafar and stopped

dead. Something opened and rose from the centre of its body.

"Not good," said Taylor.

It flashed on top and something suddenly darted towards Jafar. He raised his shield just in time as the little dart of light struck and exploded in a flash. It took a chunk out of the metal.

"Bloody hell!" Abbot hollered.

Three more shots zoomed towards Jafar, and he held his shield up so they impacted on the surface. He rushed forwards and swung his Assegai to strike it, but the nimble little thing darted out of the way and fired two more shots. One struck his shield and the other the chest plate of his armour, burning a few millimetres in. It banked around trying to strike his back when Taylor slammed in a web round magazine and fired at it. The drone was engulfed by the web and dropped down to the ground. Jafar rushed up to it and raised his leg to stamp on it.

"No! Wait!" Taylor yelled.

It was too late. Jafar's foot landed square on and crushed the drone flat to the surface. He stepped back so that Taylor could take a closer look, but Taylor was more concerned with what was coming next.

"Spread out! Take up positions!"

They all looked confused but did as ordered.

"Whatever that was, your face pissed it off!" Taylor shouted at Jafar.

"You think there are more of them?"

Taylor looked at Parker. "I think that was just an observation drone, and whoever owns it ain't gonna be too happy we just crushed their toy!"

The ground around them began groaning as if they were about to experience an earthquake, but to their surprise the ground twenty metres away began to open. But it did not split as if being torn apart. It opened in a clean fashion similar to a door.

"What have you done?" Taylor asked.

From the hole a huge metal robotic looking monster arose on an escalator until it was level with the surface. It stood three metres tall and glistened in the sun. And yet it looked nothing like Krys technology. There were few harsh lines to the armour or crude components. It looked as though crafted by an aerospace engineer. It was humanoid in shape, but with a head recessed and small in scale compared to the body.

"What on earth is that?"

"I don't know, Eli, but I'm guessing it's not friendly," said Taylor.

Lights on its head and at several points in its body lit up, and it panned around as if scanning the area. It stopped when it pinpointed Jafar, just as the little drone had. It raised its right arm and what looked like an underslung weapon built into its arm flashed. Jafar leapt quickly out of the way as the impact landed where he had stood, blowing a metre-wide crater in the ground.

"Open fire!" Taylor ordered.

He took aim and held the trigger down. His shots strafed the body of the robot but barely scratched the surface. He looked back to Jafar who was doing the same.

"Run!"

Jafar leapt into a full sprint as another explosion burst out behind him. Taylor looked to Abbot and shouted, "Get that gun firing!"

But he could see they were already rushing to get it mounted on the tripod.

As Jafar ran, the robot raised the other arm and fired with both weapons. Explosions ignited all around him, one finally striking his shield, and Jafar disappeared into a ball of light and dust. His shield had disintegrated but managed to save him. He was flat on the ground and clearly stunned. Taylor could see he was struggling to get up. He took his shield off his arm and launched it with both his hands. It flew through the air with immense speed and struck the head of the robot so hard, it caused it to stumble back a step and its shot missed Jafar by several metres.

Taylor immediately leapt into a sprint towards the robot, and it now fired on him. The shots missed him by a fraction. He jumped and used his boosters to launch himself up into the air and land atop the huge metal beast. He got a good hold onto the side of its shoulder armour and drew out his Assegai, plunging it down into the head. He stabbed it three times, but it reached up and grabbed him with an iron grip and threw him off.

He flew through the air, and his boosters had no time to break his fall. He landed hard and tumbled over several times before coming to a stop. He got up in time to see the robot take aim at Jafar once again as he was trying to get to his feet.

"Hey!" Taylor shouted.

The creature turned its face enough to look at him without moving its guns.

"Fire!" Taylor ordered.

The two 50CMGs opened fire on full auto, and the heavy rounds smashed into the creature, knocking it back as if it were being punched by something its own size. Holes were ripped into its armour, and then a single shot went right through the head. It went limp, collapsing to the ground.

Nobody said a word for a moment as they tried to take it all in. It was Abbot who finally spoke.

"Got you, you mother fucker! Woohoo!"

But as he said it, the ground rumbled, and two more hatches opened. Robots like the first one rose up from the ground. Taylor staggered over to Jafar and helped him to his feet before standing ready with their Assegais.

"Well, this isn't good."

They waited for the robots to make the first move, but

they did nothing. It was a standoff for ten seconds, and Parker whispered, "What are they waiting for?" They felt a smaller rumble in the ground that they could only imagine were more of the same giant robots coming to kill them. Instead, the ground a few metres from Taylor seemed to collapse in an organised manner and formed a stairway down beneath the surface.

"This city isn't dead," Taylor said, "Only question is, what the hell lives here?"

They waited anxiously, but did not take their hands off their weapons.

"We can't survive against many more of those things, Mitch," Parker said quietly.

"I know."

Three figures appeared from the stairway. They were as tall as Jafar but slighter built. They wore body-hugging clothing like the Mechs did beneath their armour. But this clothing seemed to be augmented with ultrafine plating and appeared as if armour that was skin fitting. Their heads were uncovered, their skin black as coal. Despite this, their facial characteristics had more in common with humans than Krys, except for flatter skulls and a much more defined and strong jawline. They seemed both terrifying, and highly intelligent and advanced at the same time.

"Who the fuck are you?" Abbot asked.

"Shhh," said Taylor, as Parker shook her head at him.

The creature at the centre finally spoke.

"This world is ours, and no other may lay claim to it. You may leave unharmed, but not that," the creature said, pointing at Jafar.

"We don't mean you any harm!" Taylor shouted.

"Then leave peacefully."

"I won't leave without my friend."

"Friend?" the creature asked in an inquisitive voice.

It seemed more surprised than anything else. It went silent as it looked at the two of them and thought.

"You stand beside them? Then you are our enemy, and you must suffer the same fate for stepping foot on this world!"

The robots' weapon systems began to power up, and visors arose out of the aliens' armours that encapsulated their faces so that they were now fully contained. Lights flashed on their forearms, and semi-translucent shields projected from a device on each of their left arms. Gun systems much like the robots used unfolded from their armour, and they took aim.

Oh, shit, thought Taylor.

He dropped the web round magazine from his rifle and slammed in a fresh regular one. He reached down for his shield and took up a stance ready to fight them, but he knew they were in deep trouble. As they were about to fire, they heard an almost deafening roar overhead as a gateway opened within the atmosphere, and a Krys vessel appeared before them.

The three aliens looked up in amazement just as they did. The ship was coming down almost right on top of them. As it did, hundreds of Mechs leapt out as its descent slowed and came down to land as Taylor's people did using assisted boosters. They landed around their position and had them completely surrounded. The aliens before them looked to Taylor as if he were the cause of it.

"You see those things? Those are my enemy!"

The creatures looked confused.

"Those are the reason we are here! We have been fighting them for years now, and we just lost our world to them!"

"But you fight alongside one?"

"He's a one in a million. They've come here to make us extinct. They are not our allies!"

He holstered his Assegai and picked up his rifle. The rest of his unit opened fire at the incoming troops.

"Kill them all!" he screamed.

CHAPTER THIRTEEN

Kelly's truck rolled into the hangar as it had a dozen times now. A crowd had gathered to greet them and cheer them on just as before. Their return was always a time for celebration. But as his truck came to a halt, the crowd could see the sombre tone on their faces. The cheering stopped when Kelly got out and climbed onto the hood to address them all.

"Today we lost friends, brothers in arms. We failed because our enemy outsmarted us. Mourn our friends who fell, but celebrate those who made it back. This is a war, and no war can be won without losses. The party goes on tonight all the same. We celebrate their lives, and we celebrate another day we are still alive!"

A few at the back started breaking out the drinks, but many stood stunned at the news. Kelly couldn't bring himself to say anymore. He knew they led a limited existence that would end bloody, but that didn't mean he had accepted the fact deep down. He climbed down and felt his back and legs tremble and feel weak. He was getting old, and there was no getting over that fact.

"You can't win them all," Becker said, passing Kelly a beer.

"That was my mission. My plan. It failed, and yet you offer me a drink?"

"We're all dead. We just don't know it yet. I'm alive right now, and that's a fact I consider worth celebrating, don't you think?"

Kelly laughed. It broke his sullen mood, and he was thankful to Becker for that. He was beginning to relax when a voice over the intercom rang out.

"We have incoming at the rear entrance. Armour and infantry."

Kelly's face turned to stone. He reached into the back of his truck, grabbed his rifle, and rushed out to the exit of the hangar.

"Everyone to your positions!" he ordered as he ran.

He got to the guardroom and found Engel supervising two of the guards observing the security screens.

"What is it? How many?"

"Sir...they appear to be..."

"What? Appear to be what?" he asked insistently.

"Human."

Becker arrived at Kelly's side in time to see an eight-wheeled armoured vehicle roll into view with three soldiers sitting atop it.

"Well, I'll be damned."

"They yours?"

"That vehicle right there is 1st Armoured Division out of Hannover. Last I heard they were fighting a hundred klicks north of here. I didn't think any of them would have made it."

"Armoured Division? That's light hardware for an armoured division?"

"Recon elements, it's probably all that made it out."

He smiled and rushed out to greet them.

"Captain!" Kelly shouted.

He stopped in surprise.

"Caution, always. We don't know yet they're who you think they are, or their intentions."

Becker's face turned more serious.

"We let you in without opposition, did we not?"

"And you were lucky we were who we said we were. It was a terrible breach of security, if you think about it."

"I'll be sure to remember that."

He carried on to the main doorway and hit the open switch. The metre-thick blast doors slid open before Kelly could reach him and say another word.

"You know the 1st?"

"One or two, not many."

"So how do we know who they really are?"

"Relax, Commander. You'll live longer."

Kelly knew Becker's carefree attitude would get them in trouble some day. He had no choice now but to wait and watch, as the vehicle column rolled into their base along the same path he had taken. It was some relief to him that they clearly knew the same route he did, but he still felt uneasy about strangers entering their compound at such a dangerous time.

Eight vehicles rode in. Many had troops atop them. They all looked exhausted and demoralised. Several of the vehicles had substantial damage caused by pulse weapons; and a couple of them were missing one or two of their wheels and yet still moving. They drew to a halt, and the troops clambered off, and others disembarked from inside the armoured transports. Not one of them said a word, but a man who was clearly their leader stepped up to Kelly and Becker. Becker showed no signs of recognising him, and he bore no rank on his uniform at all. Of if he did, it was concealed beneath the thick winter coat he wore. He did not salute nor say a word as he studied Kelly for a moment, and the Commander did likewise.

Finally, he paced up and wrapped his arms around Kelly to embrace him as a friend, despite the fact he had no idea who he was.

"Major Klein, honoured to meet you," he said, "1st Armoured."

"Commander Kelly, formerly of the MDF, and

presently of the newly founded Dragons."

Klein looked at him with a strange expression on his face.

"Dragons?"

"That is what we call ourselves. We have come together from so many places that we have decided to throw off old names and start anew. We are united as one now."

"Then will you have us? We have nothing more than what you see here. Will you let us in, and fight what's left of this war together?"

Becker couldn't believe their luck, but Kelly was still suspicious of any strangers coming into the camp. However, he looked around at the faces of Klein's people. He recognised the grim despair on their faces and knew exactly how it felt.

"Will your people stand beside mine and give it their all? Will they fight to the very end, to make the enemy suffer, until their last dying breath?" Kelly asked.

"You can be assured of that."

"Then welcome to the Drachenburg!"

There was no excitement at the prospect, only relief as Klein embraced him once again.

* * *

Taylor roared and rushed forward, leaping into the air towards one of the Mechs descending from the ship above. He fired a burst of rifle fire and struck it with his shield, causing it to tumble head first into the ground. He landed on one knee and saw another of the Mechs coming down right on top of him. He slanted his shield across his body and down the ground, held his rifle out beside it, and emptied the clip into the creature. Its lifeless body smashed into his shield and slid down the ground. He shoved it aside and got back to his feet.

"Mitch!" Parker shouted.

He looked over to see she was pointing directly above him. He looked up and saw three Juggernauts descending towards him on a triangular steel rig with thrusters built in. He rolled out of the way as it smashed to the ground, and the beasts were released.

Taylor let go of his rifle and drew out his Assegai, knowing it was the only weapon he had that was worth using now. The three Juggernauts all turned their attention to him, almost as if they had been programmed to seek him out personally. He circled them and watched their every move. He knew he was playing with fire now because he had barely survived against one of them.

Where are you, Jafar? I need you now!

One of the Juggernauts finally rushed at him, and he spun out of the way, but the beast lightly clipped his shield. As he spun, he tried to thrust with his Assegai, but the strike went wide. In the open ground they now fought, he was finding out just how fast they were in a straight line.

"Taylor!" he heard a voice yell.

It was Jafar. His deep tone was unmistakeable. He looked over. Jafar was brandishing one of the 50CMGs, and Abbot stood before him with one of the modified shields supporting the barrel. Taylor quickly ducked down, watching and listening as Jafar pulled the trigger. The gun was horrendously loud compared to anything they used as infantry. Shots ripped through the first Juggernaut and cut it down quickly. The other two quickly responded to the danger as their programming forced them to do so. They rushed towards Jafar.

The Atlantis aliens watched the situation unfold without moving. It was as if they did not fear the battle before them at all and only viewed it out of curiosity, trying to understand the history that had led to this point. Most of all, Taylor could see the one who had spoken to him watching Jafar bravely take on the Juggernauts and risk his life for Taylor.

Jafar struck down another with the heavy weapon, but it jammed as it overheated from the sustained fire. He let it drop and drew his Assegai as the last Juggernaut smashed into him and sent him flying. Taylor rushed on over to help. As he approached the Juggernaut, Jafar leapt up and struck the creature with a wild swing that hit it so hard it staggered back. As it did so, Taylor thrust his Assegai into its back.

The ferocious creature straightened and then swung

around to try and reach him. He ducked under and turned in the same direction it was turning and stabbed again. It let out a scream in pain and tried once more to reach for him, but this time Jafar got a hold of the creature and stabbed into its head. It quivered and finally dropped dead. Taylor stepped aside in time to save from being crushed by the corpse.

He nodded in appreciation to Jafar who wobbled a little, and it was clear he was still weak. Taylor took a hold of him as he dropped to one knee. He looked over to the Atlantis aliens who still watched him above all else. They seemed utterly oblivious to the battle. Pulses ignited around them, and yet somehow they were not hurt. He was not sure if they were invincible to the weapons in use, or merely mesmerised by what they saw.

Taylor looked around. The other 50CMG was still blazing away but finally jammed. The crew got to their feet and drew their Assegais and joined in the battle. He saw Abbot get hit by two pulses and another two of Parker's platoon struck down as she rushed past and engaged their attackers in hand-to-hand.

Hundreds more Mechs descended from the sky and more Juggernauts with them. Taylor knew it was far more than they could handle on their own. He looked back to the mysterious aliens who still watched the battle while their two robots stood idle like statues.

"They are the enemy!" he screamed, "Will you do

nothing?"

The three looked at each other as if trying to find consensus. They eventually looked back and began walking towards him. Still they showed no concern for their own lives. A pulse rushed towards one and past through and struck the ground with no resistance at all, neither any damage.

'They're holograms," whispered Taylor, "Just like Erdogan had been when he taunted me."

He looked down at Jafar, who was down on one knee once again and clearly wounded badly.

"I do not know who they are," he said, "But if you must give them my life in return for their help, you do it."

Taylor shook his head.

"Not a chance in hell."

He helped Jafar back to his feet and stood before the three aliens approaching them. He didn't know whether to stand in defence or offer his hand in friendship. Either way, he could tell they were far more technologically advanced than either race and should be respected as such. They stopped before him and carefully studied him and Jafar once again. The one who had spoken before addressed him again.

"These animals that invade our world. They are not your allies?"

"No, Sir," replied Taylor, "They are as far from allies as you can possibly get. We are fighting for our lives, and hopefully fighting to return to our homeworld some day."

"And this creature who fights with you. You trust him?"

"I do."

"Why?"

"Because he is my brother. He has been my brother since I met him. He has been through every hell I have been through, and been there every time for me."

"And you would risk your life for him?"

"I would. I would for any one of my people you see here."

He looked around at the battle still on going. His people were cutting down Mechs at an alarming rate, but more came to fill their place. He looked back to the three aliens, and they were still studying him. He pulled off his helmet and dropped it down by his side so they could get a better look at him. The air was putrid compared to what he was used to, but it was still nice to feel natural air on his sweaty face.

"All I want is for my people to be safe. We don't want to take anything from you, but we will take everything we can from our enemies until the very last one of us still draws breath. You seem to hate them as much as we do. Will you let them carry on ripping up your planet?"

He prayed his pleading would have some result. He didn't care for the future. All he cared about was then and there. Another fifteen minutes and they'd all be dead. One of the Mechs stormed towards him as he spoke. He ducked under as it thrust at him with its spear-like weapon and drove his Assegai deep before moving on to its comrade that followed soon after. He leapt over and turned until he landed on its back. Taylor drove his Assegai down into its collarbone, and it dropped dead beneath him.

"Please! Help us!" he shouted.

He saw a blade coming out of the corner of his eye and turned just in time for the impact to only brush his armour. Still it cut through and sliced deep into his arm. As he reeled from the pain, Jafar summoned all the strength he could and charged at the Mech and smashed it down. He punched at its faceplate until it shattered, and he struck through to its head; blood spewed out over his hands.

Taylor was on his knees, looking up at the projections of the creatures and held out his empty bloody hands.

"I beg you. Fight with us. Fight these invaders of your lands. We had no idea there were living creatures on this planet. But they did, and you know it. Help us, and we will leave here and never return. Help us to fight them!"

They looked at each other as if they were making their decision. Suddenly their projections vanished into thin air.

"No, no, no!' Taylor howled.

He got to his feet and picked up his Assegai. He tried to lift a shield with his left arm, but it had no strength left at all. He staggered over to Jafar, and wrapped his good arm around him, and helped him up to his feet.

"If we're gonna die, then we're gonna do it on our feet!"

Jafar nodded in agreement.

They turned to face two-dozen Mechs standing before them. Taylor was aching so much, he couldn't move without pain soaring through his body. It felt like the end. He wondered if this was how Chandra's life ended. He hoped it had been as honourable. But it all seemed so pointless when there would be nobody left to remember it, and nobody left to benefit from it.

Taylor looked back. Ten of their own were dead now, and several others were wounded but still on their feet. Parker's helmet was gone, and her face dripped with blood from a gushing head wound, and yet she smiled at him. She didn't say a word, and she didn't need to. He looked back at the enemy and felt the anger and adrenaline build until he felt a new power within himself.

Enough to make it a good end, he thought.

"Immortals!" he yelled, thrusting his Assegai in the air to spur them on.

He was just about to move when the two robots around them suddenly sprung into life and turned on the Mech horde. Flashes of light impacted among them as they were cut down in their droves. Three more of the robots arose to the surface and joined the fray, and then one of the black skinned aliens appeared before him. He recognised it as the one he had appealed to. This time he somehow knew it was real and not a hologram.

It said nothing but simply stared into his eyes as if

studying his every emotion. It looked back to the enemy and then leapt into action. It moved like the wind and almost floated across the ground with no resistance at all. It fired as it approached. Every single shot met its target. Every shot killed one of the enemy, and in a flash, it was in amongst their ranks. A few seconds later, it was joined by the other two who had appeared with it moments before.

"Charge!" Taylor screamed.

He rushed forward at the head of his troops. The adrenaline pumping through his veins made him forget all the pain he felt, and hope returned to his thoughts. He no longer strove for a good end, but to end every enemy daring to stand before them. Jafar carried a shield before the two of them as they advanced. The first Mech they reached turned its pulse cannon towards them, but Jafar struck it down with his shield. Taylor went past, stabbed it through the chest, and carried on without a second thought.

Taylor turned to face another opponent when he found himself looking down the barrel of a Mech pulse cannon. As the charge lit up in the barrel, he knew he had no time to move. Morris leapt in front with his shield and glanced the strike. Taylor couldn't believe his timing. It was stunning to watch as the Captain rolled forward and drove his Assegai up to its hilt. The Mech collapsed, and Morris turned to see if he was okay.

"This fight isn't over, Colonel. Come on!"

He looked around at the robots running amok through the Mechs. They stamped on some and blasted others with their arm-mounted weapons. Then he saw a flash of light, and the Atlantis aliens cutting a path through the creatures, as if they were gods fighting mere mortals. He could not help but stop and watch, as one of them darted in and out of the Mechs with such precision he had never seen. And yet it never touched the Krys with its own close quarter weapons like they did. It ducked and weaved, firing from its arm-mounted weapon, and they could seemingly never catch it.

Taylor looked back to Parker and those of his own people who were not actively fighting, as they stood over the vanquished enemies at their feet. Not one of them had a rifle in hand any longer or any ammunition left to load one. They carried their Assegais and shields only and were coated in the blood of their enemies.

"We don't die here today. They do!" he screamed, "Let's finish this!"

He rushed forward with a dozen at his side and collided with the ranks of the Mechs. Taylor thrust his Assegai from one to another. Jafar used all the strength he had left to protect him from every strike that came his way. He stabbed from left to right in a frenzy that he couldn't even control. Soon they were stepping over bodies to reach the their next victims. It was the kind of blood bath he welcomed with open arms.

Just ten minutes later they stood along the top of a mass of bodies. Forty-one of the two platoons still stood, and the three aliens who had fought them and the towering machines they controlled. They looked up at the vessel in the atmosphere above. It was being hit by shards of light that were weapons on the ground none of them could even see.

They awaited the vessel to be blown apart when a light flashed above, and it entered its own jump gate. It was still burning from the vicious hull damage. Taylor looked back across the open plain of the old city on the surface. It was scattered with bodies now, and far more of the enemy than theirs. Just one of the robots had fallen to the Krys to join the one they had felled earlier.

Taylor paced over to Jafar. He was once again down on the ground. He could barely stand, but he tried to get up as Taylor approached.

"You risked everything for me?" he asked.

"No, I did not risk it for you. You are one of the Regiment. I protect the Regiment, and to do so is to stand beside every man and woman who fights for it."

"So you would consider me one of your own? After all you have been through?"

"I will take each man and woman on their own merit. The day a horde of those Mechs turn up and offer their services, I will accept them with open arms," he jested.

Although he joked, he knew deep down he would

certainly consider it if they turned up and offered as such. Taylor slumped down and sat on the body of one of the fallen Mechs, realising how little he had left in him. He had to put effort into breathing. Morris approached and looked remarkably full of energy.

"You're getting old," he joked.

"Yes I am," replied Taylor, "but not too old to see this through."

He knew he wasn't that old yet, but he felt it. So many years of brutal combat had destroyed his body, and he was starting to feel the effects of the brutal treatment. Parker stepped towards him. The blood on her head was starting to congeal, but she appeared to have no other injury. She dropped her Assegai and fell down to wrap her arms around him.

"I thought we were dead for sure," she wept.

"We may be yet."

She pulled away from him so that she could look at his face and saw that he pointed with his eyes to the aliens they recently met on Atlantis. She had completely forgotten about the fight with their robots. It was all coming back to her now. She looked back to Taylor and shook her head.

'We can't fight them."

He nodded.

"We have enough trouble and enough enemies to fight. We cannot manage any others," she added.

'Then let's not make enemies of them."

"If it isn't too late," said Morris.

Taylor looked to his side. The Captain had been standing beside them the whole time.

"You did well today," said Taylor, "Worthy of a Captain in the Immortals."

"Just worthy?" he said with a smile.

"More than worthy. You fought like a lion. You reminded me of a friend, a brother. A brother I lost to this war."

"I am not that man."

"No, you never can be, but you can be another brother to me. There is no limit."

Morris nodded in appreciation. He knew in that moment he had finally been accepted as one of their own, in not just rank but ability also. He sat down on another of the bodies, as if it were some great relief lifted off his shoulders. Taylor reached over and touched his shoulder.

"You are as a brother to us, as Commander Kelly is a brother to me."

"If he still lives."

"Whether he lives or not, does not matter. He is a brother of mine. Though between us, if any man on Earth can survive the invasion of Erdogan, it is Kelly."

"You really believe that?"

"I do, don't you?" replied Taylor, "Honestly tell me he would just give up or walk into his own death? No. Kelly is a resourceful man. If we ever get back to Earth, I'd bet good money he'll be the one, still there and standing on the smouldering ashes of his enemies."

"If we ever do," Parker sighed.

"We thought this could ever replace Earth?" Taylor asked, "Who were we kidding? We were born to live on Earth. For whatever reason, we were born there, and it is ours. It always will be. And I intend to find a way to get back there and reclaim my home."

"How?" Parker asked.

"It's nothing more than a pipe dream," replied Morris.

Taylor looked over to the three aliens stood awaiting him. The Immortals had formed around him in a standoff against them and their robots. But they all knew they could not stand against the power of what they had seen.

"You saw how they looked at Jafar," Taylor added.

"And yet they sat by and watched as we fought and took their merry time before joining in?" asked Morris.

"I don't trust them."

"They were judging us, Parker. Waiting to see our response to the Krys. And Jafar here probably threw a spanner in the works. No wonder it took them time to come over. Wouldn't you? Most of our own race don't trust Jafar, so why would they?"

He turned to Jafar. He was starting to regain his breath but was still at only half his strength.

"They hate your kind, much like our people do. Is that a problem for you?"

Jafar shook his head.

"If they'll fight with us, I do not care."

"And if they don't want to fight with us, and they want to kill and remove us from this world?" Morris asked.

"Then we're probably fucked, Captain," replied Taylor.

He turned and looked at the three who seemed to be waiting for him to approach them. He didn't want to step any nearer than he already was, as he respected and feared their power.

"So here we are. Another alien race to come between us and the enemy we have fought all these years? We cannot afford another enemy. We can only hope they will either let us leave, or they join us."

Taylor stood up and took a deep breath, realising once again he had become a politician while in the service as a fighter. He was the only one among them willing to go forward, and it was his command anyway.

"We don't know anything about these...things."

"No, Eli, and they probably know nothing of us. Perhaps they are as wary as us, as we are of them?" Morris asked.

Parker looked to the robots standing beside them and shook her head.

"Don't think so."

"Only one question remains," Taylor said, "This fighting here today, us and them. We fought together. But were we merely allies of convenience, or are they willing to go further?"

He staggered forward, feeling the pain in his body as he told himself to put one foot in front of the other. Not one of the three aliens moved as he approached by himself.

"I am Colonel Taylor. I want my world back that those creatures took from me. All I want is to see them die and have my world back. I see you hate them just as we do. Will you fight with us?"

They looked at him for some time and then turned to each other. They seemed to communicate with their minds alone. Taylor felt his legs give out and sat down before them.

"I don't wish to fight you. You tell me when you have an answer. Tell me if you will help us save our Earth."

www.ingramcontent.com/pod-product-compliance
Lightning Source LLC
Chambersburg PA
CBHW030315200626
46816CB00006BA/1794